MEET THE MALONES

MEET
THE
MALONES

LENORA MATTINGLY WEBER

THOMAS Y. CROWELL COMPANY

New York

Published in Canada by
Fitzhenry & Whiteside Limited, Toronto

MANUFACTURED IN THE UNITED STATES OF AMERICA

Library of Congress Catalog Card No. 43-12453

ISBN 0-690-52999-6

· 25

To Larry and Tommy
who can use up paper faster and clutter up
a study floor quicker than any author

CONTENTS

MEET THE MALONES

1

Hello, Mr. Chips!

MARY FRED MALONE had just bought a horse. He was black and his name was Mr. Chips and Mary Fred was riding him home. The January wind had the moist breath of snow as it rippled the bridle reins, flapped the green scarf over Mary Fred's unruly dark hair, tugged at the end knotted under her tanned, squarish chin. She thought, "I've bought a horse." The thought could still startle her. For certainly she had not had the slightest intention of buying a horse with the money which had been sent her to buy a formal for the spring prom at school.

Mary Fred rode down the sandy road that led from the Hilltop Stables toward the outskirts of Denver, and the very rhythm of Mr. Chips' trot, the very flapping of her scarf in the wind kept time to an excited singsong inside her, "Mr. Chips is mine—all mine. He's nobody else's but mine!" And Mr. Chips' ear kept twitching back, as though he didn't want to miss a word of it. She reached over and patted his warm, black, sinewy shoulder.

Mary Fred Malone was sixteen now. She had been riding at the Hilltop Stables since she was eleven and had come out in a school club to learn to ride. All that time she had loved the black horse, Mr. Chips, with his two white forefeet and the splash of white in his forehead that someone said had started out to be a star and then fell. He was a wise and gentle horse. Their whole class had learned to ride on him, and then, later, to take the hurdles.

From the Hilltop Riding Stables to Mary Fred's home was four and a half miles. She knew because she often drove out with her chum, Lila Sears, when Lila's mother let her take her car. Lila's mother was the kind who charted every quarter-hour in Lila's life for her. "It's four and a half miles between here and the stables," she would say firmly, "so you girls can ride for an hour and then leave there promptly at five-thirty. That will give you time, Lila, to drop Mary Fred off" (for Mary Fred lived only a block from Lila), "and be home in time to change for dinner at six." And since the Japanese had fired on Pearl Harbor in early December, she always added, "Remember, our country is at war, so don't waste gasoline."

Just as Mary Fred and Mr. Chips reached the bridge which crossed the sand creek, a car's honking sounded behind them, and she pulled Mr. Chips to one side. It was Lila in her mother's roadster. If Mary Fred hadn't been riding her new purchase she would have been there in the seat beside her, dividing a candy bar.

Lila sat a moment regarding Mary Fred and her newly bought black horse, and her expression of anxiety and admiration was typical of Lila. Since they were four years old, Lila had tagged at Mary Fred's heels every minute she could escape her mother's jurisdiction, and because she was so dominated herself she worshiped Mary Fred for her unhampered initiative.

But now she said worriedly, "Honest, Mary Fred, you better change your mind and take Mr. Chips back."

"I can't," Mary Fred said with an overbright smile. "Mack said I couldn't bring him back. He said as long as I had spoiled his sale of Mr. Chips to the farmer, I'd have to stick to my bargain."

"Did you pay for him?" Lila asked.

"I paid him that fifteen dollars I had with me—you know I brought it along because we were going to shop for our formals. And I promised to finish paying Mack the other fifteen for Mr. Chips just as soon as I could."

Mary Fred and Lila had planned to meet Lila's mother at a dress shop on Colfax Avenue after their ride and start hunting for dresses to wear to the big Spring Formal in March. Lila often said that her mother stalked dress bargains with the same zest that a hunter stalked his prey.

"If only you hadn't had that fifteen dollars with you!" Lila lamented. "My grandad always said that money or a gun in your jeans could get the best-intentioned fellow into trouble. If only those doggoned old new boots of mine hadn't pinched my feet so I had to go change them and leave you there with Mr. Chips."

For it had been in those brief moments while Lila was changing out of her stiff new boots that Mary Fred had drifted over to the stall where a black head looked out wistfully.

Mack, the owner of Hilltop Stables, had explained to them that he would have to sell the horse for a low price because of a strained tendon in his right foreleg. Mack, who was a kind owner, had sighed. He hated to part with Mr.

Chips; he'd never had a horse as sweet-tempered, as generous, as understanding. The leg would be all right if it were
humored for a few months, but, because Mack had so many
clubs taking military riding, he had to fill every stall with an
active, rentable horse. He was selling Mr. Chips cheap to a
neighboring farmer.

"Why didn't you let the farmer buy him?" Lila wanted
to know.

Mary Fred took a long breath. "Well, I was standing
there by Mr. Chips' stall and he was kind of nuzzling at my
shoulder—"

"He's always been crazy about you, Mary Fred," Lila
said.

"—and this farmer came in and he was dirty and smelly
and mean—you know the kind who wouldn't even give his
kids or his wife a kind word—and he reached up and yanked
Mr. Chips' head down and started to pry open his mouth to
look at his teeth and Mr. Chips reared his head back and the
fellow cuffed him hard right on his nose and—and, honestly,
it made me sick. Sweet old Chips!"

"I know," Lila said soberly, remembering back to when
she, a scared little beginner, had climbed up on his
steady back. "I never could have taken my first hurdle
if Mr. Chips hadn't—oh, kind of promised me he'd see me
through."

A few heavy flakes of snow came sifting down. Mary
Fred stared at the fragile perfection of a frosty star on her
green-gloved hand. "You'd better go on, Lila," she said,
"and meet your mother. It's going to snow."

Lila reached for the starter, shook her head sadly. "It
worries me for you to be taking that horse home. Even
though you're a Malone. My folks would just hit the ceiling

4

—and I can't even imagine what would happen to me when they came down."

Mary Fred watched after Lila's car as Mr. Chips jogged on. Nor could she, Mary Fred, imagine what would happen to Lila if she ever did anything not previously sanctioned by her mother. Lila couldn't buy a pair of stockings without her mother at her elbow choosing the shade, deciding on the price. Lila's whole life was bordered by the phrase, "But Mother thinks—" Mary Fred remembered one time when they had been at the neighborhood store and Lila had lamb chops on her list. The butcher had no lamb chops and Mary Fred said, "Why don't you get ham?" But Lila didn't dare. She had to telephone her mother and ask what she should substitute for the lamb chops.

It had never been that way in the Malone home. The young Malones made their own decisions about lamb chops and life. "Dictators only make you soft inside," Mother used to say, and then she'd look at Father and smile, "I married in a hurry to escape dictatorship."

Mary Fred's mother had been dead three years now, but her father had the same ideas about young people making their own decisions. He wouldn't hit the ceiling when she told him she had bought a black horse. He would only say soberly, "Well, Mary Fred, if you've bought a horse, then that's your responsibility. You'll have to take care of him no matter what hardship it works upon you." She could feel his very gentle gravity; it reached through the excitement of buying Mr. Chips and riding him home.

Mr. Chips' limping became more pronounced as the miles grew. Mary Fred's happy exultancy had slowed down, too. Now the chant inside her seemed to keep time to that querulous tune, "What you goin' to do when the rent comes

5

'round?" Only the words were, "What you goin' to do when you get your horse home? What you goin' to say? How you goin' to pay?"

That was it! How was she going to pay? Fifteen dollars to Mack besides the steady output for hay and oats for Mr. Chips. She hadn't thought of that when she had said so impulsively, "I'll buy Mr. Chips."

She was almost at the city limits now, though the snow was swirling down so heavily she could see neither the university buildings nor the myriad of cozy homes she usually saw from this rise. She hated to ride a limping horse. She slid out of the saddle and walked along, leading him.

The snow kept balling up on the heels of her riding boots. Deliberately she shifted from her worried thoughts to some that were more pleasant. She remembered that this was the day her brother Johnny was to trade in his old typewriter for a newer one. She tried to walk fast for she had promised him that she'd be home in time to clean off his big old desk, which had started life as a mission table and which Johnny and she, hoping to dandy it up, had once painted blue. Yes, today was the day Johnny was to turn in his old high-busted typewriter and pay down his savings—not for a brand-new typewriter, but for one that would not skip two spaces or none at all when you hit the space bar, and would not write all the *s*'s, *m*'s, and *u*'s as capitals.

In short, Johnny's old typewriter was as unpredictable as Johnny himself. Mary Fred's fond smile became a chuckle at the thought of him. He was fifteen, a year younger than Mary Fred, and the genius of the Malone family. He could be handsome if he ever settled down to it, with his soft black eyes and endearing flash of smile. But his hair was always too long and a lank swoop of its blackness never stayed put, so

6

that his younger and more practical sister Beany was always saying, "Johnny, push your hair out of your eyes."

Johnny was a sophomore at Harkness High where Lila and Mary Fred were juniors. Johnny could write. Whenever there was an essay contest on "What America Means to Me," or "Radio in Education," other contestants grumbled, "No use us entering if Johnny Malone does." He was the delight of his English Lit teacher, gray-haired, gray-eyed, gray-garbed Miss Hewlitt. This year the school had put on a gay-nineties farce and a Christmas play, both of which Johnny had written on his space-jumping, capital-writing machine.

Again and again Johnny had been delayed in his acquiring of a better typewriter because of his half ownership in an eleven-year-old red car that was always needing a new fuel pump, or gasket, or headlight. Johnny and his friend Carlton Buell, who lived next door to the Malones, had purchased this bright red jalopy together. Although Johnny was half owner of the car, he wasn't old enough to procure a driver's license. It was often torture for him to keep his hand off the wheel and to get Carlton or Mary Fred to drive him places.

Johnny had one other trait which was a constant exasperation to his thirteen-year-old sister, Beany. He had such large-scale ideas. He could never buy a little bit of anything. If they sent him to the store for ham to fry, he would return with a whole ham. Beany never took down the pint bottle of almond extract without muttering, "That Johnny! We'll have almond extract the rest of our life, just because I asked him to get a little to flavor some icing."

The snow was coming down in great wet flurries by the time Mary Fred reached the edge of town. There was not much farther to go. She stopped and thumped her cold hands together, squirmed her foot on which the boot had rubbed a blister. Mack had given her a gunny sack half full of oats, to last Mr. Chips until she could buy some for him, and it hung with its weight divided over Mr. Chips' shoulders. She shook the clinging snow off it, too.

Mary Fred took a few steps, stopped again to reach inside her boot and pull her stocking smooth over her rubbed heel. She was leaning over with her weight against Mr. Chips' foreleg and shoulder, when through the heavy air came the screech of brakes, a woman's startled "Oh! Oh–h–h!—" and then the thudding, scraping impact of two cars coming to-gether.

Mr. Chips' startled lurch sent Mary Fred sprawling in the snow. Scrambling up quickly, she blinked the snow off her eyelashes and looked in the direction of the sounds. She gave a shocked and frightened cry. She pulled hard at the unwilling horse as she ran forward.

2

The Fractured Eggs

THROUGH the veil of snow several things leaped out at Mary Fred. First Johnny's and Carlton's red car sitting sideways in the road with its front fenders folded under. And there was Johnny picking something off the ground. She came closer and saw the rest of the picture.

A small truck with a Wyoming license plate had evidently been hit, and the jolt had knocked one egg case out on the ground and tipped the other over in the back of the truck. It was eggs that Johnny was picking up, looking miserable and unkempt and with the snow coating his black shock of hair.

And there was the woman who had screamed out, "Oh! Oh–h–h!" She was sitting on the running board of the Wyoming truck, crying. She was holding her handkerchief to her mouth as though there was something about her teeth she wanted to hide.

Suddenly another figure, who must have been bending over on the other side of the truck, straightened up, and his hands, too, were full of eggs. Mary Fred stared at him. He looked a little like a picture of a cowboy in a rodeo advertisement, only more sober-hued. He wasn't wearing a doeskin vest, plaid shirt, and fringed chaps, but you felt they belonged on him by the very swing to his body and the extra breadth to his hat brim, by the farsighted look in his eyes which seemed startlingly blue in his bronze face. He stooped over again to get some eggs that had rolled halfway under the truck.

Mary Fred could almost fill in the details of what had happened. For some reason Carlton, the lawful driver of the car, had been detained at school; and Johnny, all eagerness to put through his typewriter deal, had driven home, picked up his old typewriter and his savings, and set out for school so that Carlton could drive them downtown. Yes, there sat his old dilapidated typewriter on the seat of the red car.

Mary Fred guided Mr. Chips so he wouldn't step on the spilled eggs. She said, "Gosh, Johnny, what happened?"

"Why hello, Mary Fred. It—it was all my fault," he admitted. "I turned right in front of them. I should have been more careful. I guess I was thinking of something else."

Mary Fred groaned inwardly, "I guess you were, Johnny —you're always thinking of something else."

Mary Fred asked the crying woman, "Are you hurt?"

"No," she said, "only I'm kind of shook-up—seeing all those eggs spilled and broken that I've been saving so long. I was bringing in two cases of them to pay the dentist for some work I have to have done."

Johnny said quickly, "I'll pay for the eggs. How much did you figure you'd get for them? I'll take them all home— some are only a little bit cracked, and a few are still in one piece. Our family likes eggs. And I'll pay for the damages to your car, too."

The shrill of a siren interrupted. A police car skidded to a stop across the street and two bulky representatives of the law got out. Their blue uniforms loomed up ominously through the blur of snow. Mary Fred's heart pounded in dread. Just let them find out that Johnny was driving without a license!

The first terse question was the same one Mary Fred had asked, "What happened here?"

The tall young cowboy stepped forward. "We've just about got it settled between us. I don't believe you'll need to make any record of the case. There's no harm done and no one hurt."

"I'm going to pay for the eggs," Johnny put in.

For one awful minute Mary Fred thought she saw the policeman's eyes measuring Johnny's tall immaturity and that she'd hear him snap out, "You're not more than fifteen, are you? Let's see your driver's license." But instead he said relievedly, "That's the best way to do—settle it between yourselves. Take it to court and there's a lot of time and money wasted. There's more automobile accidents with nobody willing to take any blame." He looked at the sniffling woman, then at the young cowboy. "This your mother here? You ain't hurt are you, lady?"

The woman answered, "No, I'm not his mother. My husband is foreman of his father's ranch. It's my truck, and my eggs. Ander drove it in for me because he was coming in to school here. I'm not hurt—I'm just, you might say, shook-up." And she repeated with her hand shielding her mouth, "I was bringing in these eggs to pay the dentist for some work I have to get done."

The second policeman said, "Sure you can settle every-thing between you?" Everyone concerned nodded and he said, "Okay then. Come on, Mullen, we'll catch that new call."

Mary Fred stood beside Johnny and watched with relief as the police car glided off through the snow. Johnny turned to the young man from Wyoming—Ander, the woman called him. "Whew–w–w! Thanks! That sure kept me from be-ing on the spot."

Ander laughed, "That's what I figured."

Mary Fred asked, "How many eggs are there in each case?"

"Twenty-four dozen. Forty-eight dozen in both," the woman answered.

"And what are they worth a dozen?" Johnny asked smally.

"Twenty-nine cents," Ander answered. "I had my aunt who lives here in town ask her grocer. That's why Mrs. Thompson brought them in—because she can get more for them here than in Wyoming."

Mary Fred saw Johnny's lips moving as he tried to figure in his mind how much forty-eight times twenty-nine was. He must have got some idea, for he gave a sigh that was like the heave of a horse and he looked at his old derelict type-writer with the sick realization that he must give up all thought of getting a newer one.

But he continued valiantly, "How much do you figure it'll cost to iron out the fender and get a new light put in? I've got enough on me to pay for the eggs. But you'll have to trust me for the repairs."

"Of course, I'll trust you," the woman said simply. "I can tell your word is good. I'll get the car fixed up in Wyoming where we come from and they'll do it reasonable. And you can pay us when you get it."

Ander suddenly became aware of Mary Fred and the black horse moving restlessly in the background. He asked her sharply, "Did you ride that horse so hard you lamed him?"

"I did not," she answered even more sharply.

"Whose horse is it?"

"He's mine."

The Wyoming boy bent over the horse, felt tenderly along the lame leg. "Tell you what you do for him. You get on home just as soon as you can and put a hot pack on his leg here where it's swollen. Then about three packs a day will ease it down. You've no business having him out in this driving snow. It's slippery going—he's liable to strain it still more."

The reproof in his voice angered Mary Fred. As though she were dawdling about in the snow with a limping horse on some whim of hers! She started to say, "I'll go home as fast as I can with a couple of blistered heels." But she had to close her lips in swift panic and turn her head. How unbelievably silly! To feel your lips go wabbly and a surge of tears threatening. Just because she was cold and tired and worried about taking home the horse, and her heels were rubbed raw, and she was, like Mrs. Thompson, "shook-up" by the accident, was no reason for her to go 1890 and burst into tears when a blue-eyed cowboy from Wyoming criticized her.

But she turned away, tugged heavily on Mr. Chips' reins and, without a word, left the scene, thankful for the curtain of snow, sheer at first like dotted marquisette, but thickening into a white cloud as the distance grew between them.

Dusk was already sifting through the polka-dotted veil of snow. She was afraid the oats would get wet with the snow caking over the porous sack on the horse's back. So she brushed the snow off the sack and carried it under her arm.

She turned down her own Barberry Street. There were three big houses in their block: the gray-stone Malone house in the middle, the home of Johnny's chum Carlton Buell on the far side, and the house Mary Fred was just passing in which lived Mrs. Morrison Adams.

Mary Fred peered through the snow at her own home. No, the front part of the house wasn't lighted. Thank goodness, Father wasn't home yet! She preferred breaking the news of her purchase in a more gentle way than for him to see her leading home a badly limping horse.

The home of Mrs. Morrison Adams was imposing red brick with immaculate white trimming. Since their mother's death the Malones had a housekeeper whose name was also Mrs. Adams. To avoid confusion they distinguished between the two by calling the one in their home Mrs. No-Complaint Adams (although she told of the different places she had worked, there had never been a word of complaint about her work) and the other Mrs. Socially-Prominent Adams (on the society page she was always referred to as that).

As Mary Fred passed, Mrs. Adams was just being escorted to her waiting car by her chauffeur. He was holding an umbrella over her to protect her hair-do and her costume from the wet snow, and Mrs. Adams was holding up the skirt of her dinner dress with one hand and carrying in the other her little fluff of Pekinese by name of Tiffin. To date the excitable Tiffin had never let a Malone pass without running out and barking in shrill defiance and nipping at his or her heels.

Mrs. Adams paused to look at Mary Fred, sploshing stiffly through the snow in boots that were rubbing both heels unbearably, carrying an awkward load in a gunny sack under her arm, and leading a limping horse. Mrs. Adams' expression said, "What will those awful Malones bring home next?" And at the same time Tiffin leaped from his mistress's arms and ran, with a crescendo of shrill barking, at Mr. Chips.

The black horse deigned one annoyed look backward, then administered, not viciously but in an I'm-doing-this-for-your-own-good manner, a kick that sent Tiffin sprawling and yelping in the muddy slush. Mary Fred thought with satisfaction, "Someone is going to have to clean Tiffin up before he can mingle with the socially prominent tonight."

At the same time the Malone dog, Red, came trotting out to meet them. Mr. Chips he knew and liked because Mary Fred often took Red to the stable, and he greeted the horse with his customary dignity and restraint. It annoyed Beany Malone that, while all the young Malones loved to turn and stamp and threaten Tiffin and grumble about his vicious enmity, there were two in the Malone family who refused to admit he existed. One was Father, who walked down the street and never seemed to know that a little bundle of dog was having hysterics at his pants leg, and the other was their dog Red, who trotted by, his big-dog dignity never permitting even a glance toward all the sound and fury that was Tiffin.

The stone garage on the Malone place had once been a stable before modern transportation had forced the Malones to remove the mangers and the partitions and replace the wooden floor with concrete. Mr. Chips slid on the smooth concrete as Mary Fred coaxed him in. First she had to tap out and pry loose the snow caked around his shoes.

Again uneasiness, sharper this time, went through Mary Fred. The horse looked so big, so almost *raw* here beside the metalic gleam of their car. She wondered where she'd get straw for bedding and hay to feed him. She wished there was something to tie him to. With cold, shaking hands she pulled the saddle off him, unbridled him—yes, and she wished there were a peg to put the saddle on.

She put it on top of the car hood and there in the dusk it looked like a rakish little hat. She emptied piled newspapers out of a carton and shook a feeding of oats into it. Mr. Chips could hardly eat for looking about curiously. There was no bucket for water except one that smelled faintly of gasoline. She'd have to scour it out. Later, too, she must see about those hot compresses. She wished the bossy boy from Wyoming had told her how to make them.

She stamped her way up the back-porch steps. The kitchen door opened and Mrs. Adams came out, wrapped in her heavy coat and tying a knitted scarf under her chin. "I have to hurry along to get the supper going at my daughter's. Did you interview the woman I told you about, Mary Fred —the one who said she allowed she could take my place?"

Mary Fred was doubled over in the porch doorway with one boot in her hand, knocking the snow off it. She straightened and said, "Land of love! I knew there was something else I should have done. I was going to interview her after Lila and I looked at dresses. And then—then so many things happened. I forgot all about seeing her."

Mrs. Adams tch-tch'd her disgust and reproach. "You know my time was up yesterday. I came over today to cook you up enough to carry you over a day."

"I know," Mary Fred said, and murmured her thanks

16

and appreciation for Mrs. Adams' giving them an extra day out of the kindness of her heart. Mrs. Adams' daughter had obtained work at the munitions plant and Mrs. Adams was leaving the Malones to care for her daughter's home and children.

"Dear knows, you Malones will need someone. I never saw such slug-abeds in the morning, and there's your poor father having to have his hot filling breakfast right on the dot. Oh, but he's the fine one and a pleasure to work for. As I said to my daughter, 'I've known smart people and I've known good people but you don't often find smart people good or good people smart—but you'd never find anyone as good and as smart as Martie Malone.' What would this town do without him and his writin' on the paper? Why, Mary Fred, he does the thinking for all of us as haven't much to think with. He does, indeed! He thinks things out about all that's goin' on in the world and then he puts it in his—what do you call it now, Mary Fred?"

"His editorial column," Mary Fred said, shaking the snow off the scarf that had only partially protected her head and neck.

"That's it—and written so plain and nice that most times I can understand it. And my daughter says that they have the school children read what he writes in this class they call —what is it now, Mary Fred?"

"Current Events," Mary Fred said, and felt again the proud thrill she had always felt when she saw written on the school blackboard, "Read Martie Malone's column on 'Inside America.'"

As Mrs. Adams talked she was pulling down a few garments she had washed and hung on the porch clothesline, and now she wadded them into Mary Fred's arms. "These are to be ironed, Mary Fred. Now see that you dampen them down good."

The woman started down the snowy steps, stopped to call back, "The dinner's in the oven, but you'll have to dish up yourself. You should have seen about hiring that woman."

Mary Fred stared after Mrs. Adams' figure that was of the same solid bulk as Mrs. Socially-Prominent Adams. A great inspiration was forming in Mary Fred's mind in answer to the worrying singsong of "What you goin' to pay?" A new line had even added itself, "He'll need oats and hay."

Why couldn't the young Malones do the housework and the cooking and the laundry which Mrs. Adams had done so capably? It would mean getting up earlier each morning and hurrying home from school each afternoon. Already some days seemed full to overflowing. But here was Mary Fred with a horse to finish paying for and feed to buy. Here was Johnny in just as much of a jam with the repairs on the Wyoming truck to pay for.

Why couldn't the three of them, Johnny, Beany, and Mary Fred, divide the work? She felt a good-sized qualm of doubt as to how useful Johnny would be around the house. Beany was only thirteen, but Beany had a God-given instinct about draining noodles without spilling them in the sink and beating the lumps out of white sauce with an egg-beater, while Johnny—Johnny couldn't even put the percolator together in chronological order.

Why couldn't they hold a council table this evening and thresh over with Father the problems attending the purchase of a lame black horse and the collision with a truck carrying eggs to the market?

3

Beany Tells
Her Heart's Desire

MARY FRED opened the kitchen door. Thirteen-year-old
Beany, who had been christened Catherine Cecilia but who
was only called that by her teachers, was there. She was
kneeling on a chair at the kitchen table looking over her
cooking-class notebook. Her hair, which she wore in thick
braids, was just losing the towheadedness of childhood. Her
round face was ruddy and resolute. Beany was easily the
most practical of the Malones. She said, "We've got to make
some doughnuts. This recipe doubled makes five dozen plus
twenty. Don't you know we promised to take five dozen
down to the rookie center every Saturday morning?"

Mary Fred didn't answer that. Her mind was still following the inspired trail on which necessity had driven it.
"Beany," she asked, "is there something you want so bad you
can taste it?"

"Is there!" Beany looked up from the loose-leaf notebook and her eyes grew rapt with longing. "Oh, Mary Fred,
wait till I show you." She scurried into the hall and came

back with her arithmetic book and from it drew a folded magazine page. She unfolded it from creases that were worn through in places and held up before Mary Fred a picture of a girl's bedroom with a description which was captioned, "Bring Sun and Space into that Small North Room."

Beany said slowly, "Nobody knows how I loathe that room of mine with that nursery wallpaper and that stinking border of rabbits around it."

Mary Fred, wriggling her cold toes in their dampish socks, remembered guiltily that before Mother died she had said, "We *must* do over Beany's room!" The room which Mary Fred occupied and which she and her older sister Elizabeth had originally shared was really a two-room suite; one room could be either a bedroom or upstairs sitting room, for it had a fireplace in it, and off it was a porch with glassed-in, sliding windows on three sides. Beany's room, which was next to the bedroom, had originally been a small nursery room.

Mary Fred pushed in Beany's loose side comb and said, "Why don't you move into my room with me, Beany? Your room *is* pretty dinky."

"I like my own room even if it is dinky," Beany said. "Only it just insults a girl of my age to look up in the morning and see a border of rabbits tending the flowers—especially that one rabbit with glasses and a fatherly expression."

Mary Fred was studying the picture room. "Beany, why don't you do your room over like this?"

"I kind of thought about it—but I was kind of scared that maybe it wouldn't look right. But see, it says here: 'All these things can be accomplished by a pair of deft hands . . .'"

"Well, if you haven't got deft hands, I never saw any. Didn't you get A on your Home Ec project? You could make those ruffled curtains. And why couldn't you paint your bed? And we could take the mirror off your dresser. Of course you could do your room over scrumpy!"

Beany looked at her older sister's face as though she needed to draw from it the confidence that said, "Go ahead." Beany said slowly, "Our sewing machine has a ruffler—and I always wanted to ruffle with it. Yessir, Mary Fred, I'll bet I could do my room over. Listen, here's what it says: 'These yellow-plaid curtains will lift the sun right out of the sky and bring it into the room.' And here's what it says about bringing space by treatment of the walls. It says: 'Some decorators still hold to the belief that blue is a cold color for walls, but not in this small room. Imagine, if you can, a shade halfway between robin's egg blue and the sky in August, which poets claim is the color of the Virgin Mary's robe.' You see," Beany added, "you get the warmth and yet the restfulness of space. You really do think I could do it myself, don't you, Mary Fred?"

"Of course, you could," Mary Fred assured her. "As Mrs. No-Complaint Adams says, you're more-handier than any girl your age."

Beany went on happily, "Oh, then I wouldn't need to be ashamed to bring a girl home to stay all night with me. Honest, Mary Fred, it does something to my soul to look up the first thing in the morning and see those rabbits looking down at me. I never did like rabbits. Not even Frank—not even if he does try to win me by making faces at me."

When Beany was ten a friend of Father's had given her a small white rabbit for Easter. "At first," Beany often lamented, "he seemed too young to get rid of. And now— well—now he seems too old and peculiar." Frank was, in-deed, less timid than others of his species. He was always getting out of his cage. He preferred the safety and coziness under the back steps to his box cage with its wire front. Perhaps Frank realized and appreciated that he owed his safety to Red, who saw to it that all stray dogs were kept out of the yard on those occasions when Frank was at large.

Mary Fred was thinking aloud, "We paid Mrs. No-Complaint Adams forty a month and Father gave her sixty for the groceries. How much is forty divided by three, Beany?"

"Thirteen and a third. Why?"

Mary Fred's mind was coping with the price of oats and baled hay and the payment of the fifteen-dollar balance to Mack at the Crestwood Stables. "We'll thresh it all out at the council table tonight, my pet," she said.

She realized then she was still holding the dry clothes which Mrs. Adams had stuffed into her arms, and she deposited them on the table.

The top garment was a turquoise linen blouse which had belonged to their older sister Elizabeth, until she had given it to Beany to wear with her plaid jumper. Mary Fred had a sudden picture of Elizabeth standing in the hall running a comb through her lovely light hair, wearing this turquoise blouse and her flame-red suit, and she knew a homesick longing for her. She said, "Oh, Beany, don't you wish the door would open and Elizabeth would yell out 'Hi, my handsomes!' like she used to?"

But last spring Elizabeth had been married to tall, broadshouldered Lieutenant Donald MacCallin with his warm, likable smile. They had hurried off to his army post. This last year Elizabeth's letters had borne postmarks from three, no, four different army camps. But she had promised them all that when Donald was sent overseas she would come home again.

Beany said wistfully, "Whenever I read in a book, 'Her hair was an aureole about her face,' I think of Elizabeth. Hers was, wasn't it, Mary Fred?"

"Um-hmm, just exactly. And just halfway between gold and auburn." Mary Fred sighed a little as she sprinkled the turquoise blouse. Elizabeth was so lovely. When she had graduated from Harkness High they wrote under her picture in the yearbook, "She is debonair and pretty; she is full of pep and witty—and how we love her!" Her first year at college, Elizabeth had been chosen freshman escort for the campus queen during Homecoming Week. Mary Fred remembered the boxes of roses, the incessant telephone calls, the poems about love and spring that Elizabeth elicited. Mary Fred's sigh was unformed regret that she was not the glamour-girl type.

Mary Fred asked, "Was there a letter from Elizabeth today?"

Beany shook her head. "Nope."

Mixed with Mary Fred's homesickness for Elizabeth was a tinge of uneasiness. She knew something about Elizabeth that the rest of the family did not. Elizabeth had written a special letter to her: "There's going to be a baby, Mary Fred, and so I won't be too desolate when Don has to leave. Be thinking up names for it, and don't tell Father yet. You know how he'd worry about me trekking along after Don at army camps—but every minute together before he goes is pretty precious."

The telephone rang, and Beany and Mary Fred looked at each other and said almost simultaneously, "Oh—oh, that's Father—and it means company!"

Father's friends were legion. Martie Malone had been a court reporter as well as a sports writer before he became

23

city editor of Denver's afternoon paper, where he now wrote the editorials which a hundred and seventy thousand subscribers discussed over dinner tables and in street cars, and which school children gave reports on in their Current Events classes.

"Call out and tell me whether I should set the table with the Haviland or the blue pottery," Beany prompted Mary Fred. It was more usual than not for the telephone to ring about this time of evening and for Martie Malone to say, "Put another plate on—I'm bringing someone home."

If it was a lady—perhaps a journalist or a champion swimmer or a W.C.T.U. lecturer—Beany set the table with their Ranson rose Haviland with its paper-thin, flowerlike cups. But if it was a man—an escaped refugee, the heavyweight boxing contender, an Irish poet—then they put on the blue pottery because men like coffee out of thick cups and it didn't bother Beany to see them mash out cigarettes in the pottery saucers.

It was Father's deep, genial voice that said, "Hello, sprout!"

"Company?" Mary Fred asked. "Male or female?"

Father answered, "I thought maybe he was there already. I sent him out. Hasn't old Emerson Worth arrived yet?"

"Not yet."

"He's down in the dumps, honey, and cantankerous as a goat. I don't think he's had a square meal for a couple of days. He was pretty shaky when I sent him out."

"Oh gosh!" Mary Fred sighed.

"Poor old Emerson," her father said gently, and Mary Fred knew from his very tone that he was reminding her that Emerson Worth was once a famous newspaper man who had extended a friendly hand to Martie Malone when he had started out. He wanted her to remember that old Emerson was now destitute and alone, with his once fine mind at times so bitter, at times so wandery, that it was all Martie Malone could do to keep him on a routine job at the *Call* where Martie was editor. Father added, "He needs a hot meal and a little building up."

Martie Malone and the young Malones were in a conspiracy to boost up the old man's limp ego. No one knew the history of Denver or of the West as well as Emerson Worth, who had been part of the city's building. He believed that the men, women, and children of those early days were of sturdier stuff than the people of the present. And he resented it because these same *weaklings* of today weren't even interested in hearing about the lusty giants who moved through those lusty old days.

So Martie Malone often pretended that he needed Emerson Worth's help on a column he was writing that dealt with historical fact. Or sometimes one of the children—Johnny usually—pretended he needed early-day data, which only Emerson Worth could supply, to use in a school assignment.

Mary Fred asked, "Of what historic event must we pretend to crave knowledge?"

Father laughed as he answered, "It's General Sherman's arrival in Denver in the late '60's. I told him you children wanted to know all about it."

Oh, land of love, Mary Fred thought, as though life weren't complex enough with a horse, just half paid for, out in the garage and the news still to be broken to the family, and Johnny just now driving in with his two wrecked and spilly cases of eggs, and Mrs. Adams leaving, and five dozen doughnuts to be made tonight so Father could take them to the rookie recreation center in the morning, and she, Mary

Fred, with a blister on each heel! And now Emerson Worth would be coming in, shaky and wandery, and telling of how "giants walked the streets in those days." And they must pretend great interest in every detail of the banquet held for General Sherman when he toured the West.

"He may not want to come in," Father said. "This is one of his bitter days when he thinks no door will open to him. But get him in, and give him a cup of hot coffee to brace him up."

"Okay," Mary Fred promised, "we'll entice him in and brace him up."

Out in the kitchen she put one of Mrs. Adams' cellophane aprons over her plaid flannel shirt and green riding pants, slid her tired feet into flapping-soled huarachos, and she and Beany attacked the doughnut recipe. And here they had their first experience with Johnny's cracked and leaking eggs —"those fractional eggs," sometimes "those fractured eggs," as Beany was to term them. "How can you tell," Beany's mathematical mind would argue, "how many to use when some are only half an egg, some are only a fourth—and some are only a suggestion of what was once an egg?"

The doorbell rang just as Mary Fred was rolling out the first batch of doughnuts and Beany was saying of the skillet of fat, "It's smoking."

"There's Dad's company now," Mary Fred said, forgetting that Beany didn't know that she and her father had discussed Emerson Worth's arriving. "Answer the door, Beany. And get him in the house if you have to drag him in. Only hurry up, because the grease is sizzling."

Beany returned promptly to the kitchen with her report. "He didn't want to come in. I all but pushed him into the front room."

26

The doughnuts were on their last lap with only two more skillets full to fry by the time the coffee had percolated to dark, fragrant strength. Mary Fred poured a cup, went through the dining room and into the big front room which opened off the hall. It was gray-dark in the room. Beany shouldn't have been in such a hurry as not to turn on the light! Mary Fred groped for it with one hand while she balanced the full coffee cup on its saucer and said, "Here now, drink a cup of hot coffee before Father comes. It'll warm you up. We were just hoping you'd come out and tell us about Sherman."

And then she stared about the lighted room in unbelief—not at one occupant of the room, but at two. Old Emerson Worth was there on a corner of the couch. He had evidently been there for some time, for even though he was holding his shapeless hat on his knee and his white silk scarf was still wrapped about his neck and tucked under his damp, shabby overcoat, he was snoring in tired old-man oblivion. And sitting on the edge of the chair nearest the door was the tall young man whose eyes seemed all the bluer for being in his dark, wind-tanned face.

He stood up, tall, lean, carelessly graceful. Even as Mary Fred had known, his hair was light. It was Ander of the egg disaster. He gave a low chuckle; it was easy and casual and refreshing as the rolling distances of Wyoming. "All I can tell you about Sherman is that one famous remark of his about war," he said.

Mary Fred laughed sheepishly. "You must think we're an outlandish lot. First my brother knocks the car you're driving off the road, and then you come to the door—I don't know why you came—and my sister drags you in by force. We have a neighbor, Mrs. Socially-Prominent Adams, who thinks we're the awful Malones." If Mary Fred hadn't been rattling on in embarrassed fashion she might have noticed that he gave her an odd look. "Did you come to see Johnny about the bashed truck and the eggs?"

"No, he and Mrs. Thompson made all the arrangements about that. I didn't even know Johnny lived here. I just stopped at the door to see if I was on the right street. I came to stay at my aunt's and go to Medical, but there wasn't anyone home and I couldn't see the name of the street for the snow against the curb."

"Oh—you're going to Medical?"

"Yes. I came down from Wyoming because I can make better time here. I can go straight through this summer. I want to get through soon's I can so as to be ready for army service."

"What street does your aunt live on?"

"On Barberry Street."

"What's her name?"

He smoothed his chuckle into a smile. "Mrs. Adams," he said. "I believe you call her Mrs. Socially-Prominent Adams."

"Oh dear—oh dear!" Mary Fred said weakly. She was suddenly conscious of her flour-smudged, transparent apron over her damp, mussed riding clothes, of the huarachos flapping at the end of riding pants that were meant for boots. But he seemed to be thinking of something else. "Did you put that hot pack on your horse's lame leg?"

"No—I didn't know exactly how to."

"I'll fix it for you." He got to his feet.

"No—no, let's wait. I hear Father coming. Right after dinner we can."

4

The New Regime

ANDER ERHART stayed to dinner at the Malones and, like all the evening meals where Martie Malone sat at the head of the table and Beany watched over the coffee cups and the milk pitcher and the bread plate, it was informal, relaxing, and stimulating.

Emerson Worth had brought out the menu of that old-time General Sherman banquet, the big event of 1866. "My aunt was there," he related. "What a time the women had getting their ball dresses ready when there were only a few sewing machines in town. They had to take turns at them. And the town was sold out of neckties. My aunt said she had to make my uncle one. Now here's what they had for side dishes."

They all read the menu yellowed with age:

SIDE DISHES

Picade of Mutton, garnished with Jelly, Smothered Duck, Port Wine Sauce. Gallatine of Turkey,

Aspig Jelly. Bone Chicken, stuffed with Oysters.
Pig's Head, a la Anglaise, with Lobster. Mutton
Cutlets, Current Jelly. Glazed Calf's Head, stuffed
with Mushrooms. Mutton Chops, a la Bordaloise
Sauce. Spiced Tongue, Egg Sauce. Scollopped Oys-
ters, Frills of Brown Bread. Veal, a la Pasco,
Marinal's Sauce. Fried Oysters. Scollopped Brains,
cruscades of Brown Bread.

Father said, "I hope everyone had access to bicarb of
soda."

"Did they serve them all?" Beany asked awed. "Or is
it like our menus with 'or' between each one?"

"They served them all," Emerson Worth said grandly.

"Quite a little waddin'," Ander commented.

"And these were the cakes they served," Emerson Worth
said:

Jelly, Small Fruit, Amulets eu fra, Pyramid Cakes,
Cookies, a la franz, Pound. Fancy Fruit, English
Copays, Diamond Ice, Strawberry Cake, Metro-
politan, plain. Plain Pound.

Johnny said, "Beany, haven't we got some doughnuts, à
la Malone?"

Beany went for a plateful. She had figured out that by
doubling their recipe they could make the soldier boys their
five dozen and still have enough for the Malones for dinner
at night and breakfast in the morning. She stood there with
the plate of doughnuts in her hand, staring transfixed at the
window. "There's a horse looking in at us. Look, all of you."

Ander said, "He must be thirsty—he's eating the snow off

the window sill." (Mary Fred remembered that she had *intended* scrubbing out a pail and giving him water.)

Father looked interestedly at the black head with the splash of white in its forehead. "Well, we've often attracted dogs or cats, a rabbit, and a turtle now and then, but this is the first stray horse that's come scratching to be let in."

Mary Fred said in a small voice, "That's my Mr. Chips." She felt the avalanche of questions gathering in Beany, so she hurried on, "I bought him—at least he's one-half bought. I paid down my formal money and I still owe Mack fifteen and I have to pay it as soon as I can. Mack said Mr. Chips only needed a few months' rest to be good as new. And when he's all right Mack will take him back and board him. He can rent him out enough over week ends to pay for his board, but he'll still be mine to ride through the week."

Father had followed attentively. "And how do you plan to pay for your Mr. Chips and buy his oats and alfalfa?"

"I was wondering," Mary Fred stammered, "because Johnny, Beany, and I all need to earn some money—"

"I *got* to," Johnny put in unhappily. "I paid for the eggs with my typewriter money but I still got the bashed light and fender to pay for." Rather incoherently at first, but finally becoming understandable with Ander and Mary Fred adding details, the story of Johnny's accident came out.

Father said thoughtfully, "Yes, I'd say you did have to dig up some money, you two. Beany, what about you? You didn't buy a giant panda or wreck a tank, did you?"

"It's those stinky rabbits in my room I want to get rid of," Beany said earnestly. "I want to do it over and bring sun and space into it." She hurried to get the picture to show them all. Her eyes grew visionary as she computed how many yards of yellow-plaid gingham it would take, as she

31

told of the shade of blue for the walls that was to be half-way between robin's egg blue and the gray-blue of an August sky which was the blue of the madonna's robe.

Father looked at them all, then at Ander and at old Emerson Worth, and he smiled with appealing helplessness. "It's times like these that are tough on parents," he said. "I ache to give Mary Fred the money for her horse, and get Johnny out of his mess and say, 'Beany, hop to it and get what you need.' It'd give me the same pleasure it gives a hen to spread her wings over her chicks. But I can't manage it, and my reason tells me it's a blessing I can't. Their mother and I believed that they'd have no chance of growing if they were always protected."

Emerson Worth quoted from the man for whom he was named, " 'The highest price you can pay for a thing is to get it for nothing.' That's the trouble with this generation; they want everything—"

Mary Fred interrupted before the old man could launch out on his pet theme. "Why couldn't we three do Mrs. Adams' work instead of hiring another woman? We could keep the house clean and get the meals and all that."

"And go thirty-three-and-a-third on the money," put in Beany.

"You mean mop the floors and wash and cook—oh gosh!" Johnny murmured.

The very way he said it chilled Mary Fred's ardor momentarily. They'd have to watch that Johnny didn't do the marketing.

Beany said severely, "You'll just have to put your mind to it and work hard if you want to get your share of the housekeeping money."

And so a council was held.

Emerson Worth was banging on the table, orating, "This is a democracy where free men speak, where every voice is heard." And Ander was saying, "I can help you get your black horse in shape, Mary Fred; I've coddled many a bronc till he got cured of strained tendons."

Father took his usual time hunting his pipe. He said as he tapped it thoughtfully on the palm of his hand, "These days when we're at war are serious days. We can't waste food. We need filling meals to stand by us. If you children take over and claim the forty dollars the job is worth, it means you must give value received. It doesn't mean that you can get by in the easiest possible way. Do you realize it means getting up earlier than you have been to get breakfast, and put up school lunches? And for dinner none of your wienies on buns and a handful of potato chips."

"We're studying economical meals in domestic science," Beany said eagerly.

"So are we," put in Mary Fred, and wished she had given more heed to them.

Father was filling the pipe now, cupping a finger around the bowl while he shook the tobacco in. "Any equipment you break or put out of commission you'll have to replace. If it's a choice between dates and your work here, this work comes first. We don't want a slipshod home. We want one that's a pleasure for folks to come to. And we want to keep it open to soldiers and all who don't have one of their own."

They sat soberly watching him strike the match, hold it a careful distance from the tobacco. The tobacco flared red and Father blew out a happy breath of smoke to extinguish the match. "So," he said, his gray eyes both teasing and steadying them, "if you do solemnly pledge to do the work, I'm willing to let you take it over and pay you the money."

"We'll work like billy-goats," Mary Fred promised him.

Emerson Worth quoted further, " 'What wilt thou?' quoth God. 'Take it and pay for it.' I set type for so many years. I saw stories made by big people, little people. The ones who thought they could get everything for nothing. But they weren't the ones who built the State."

Mary Fred said, "Our Miss Hewlitt says it's a great pity someone doesn't write the history of our State while some of the people who lived it are still with us. The school calls it her battle cry—'Write an intimate history of Colorado.' She's taught for thirty years, she says, and she's still hoping to inspire someone to do it. Johnny, why don't you help Emerson write it? You could, Johnny, you with your gift for writing. And Emerson knowing Buffalo Bill and Chief Colorow."

"I always planned to write it," the old man said shakily, "but somehow the years crept up on me."

Mary Fred said in a voice so low it couldn't reach his old ears, "You could be Emerson's prodder-on, Johnny."

And Beany added in the same low voice, "And you could be Johnny's prodder-on, Mary Fred."

Johnny stood up and his chair fell with a clatter behind him. But Johnny didn't hear it. His eyes had a faraway light, like a beacon on a distant hill. "Sure, we could, Emerson," he said softly. "It was your uncle—you've told me yourself—who came across the plains with his shirttail full of type. All the things you've told us—about the town starting from a little bunch of log shanties, and the miners coming in and pinching out gold dust to pay for things and that's how the terms two bits and four bits got started—"

Martie Malone said, "You've got something there, you two."

Beany said anxiously, "But, Johnny, you've got to remember to put water in the lower part of the double boiler when you cook."

But Johnny didn't hear that either. "I'm going to telephone Miss Hewlitt and tell her."

Ander looked at Mary Fred as he got up from the table. "Let's get your cayuse watered, dosed, and bedded down."

They left Beany a plump bundle of happiness and plans. She offered to take the first third of the month and do the cooking while Johnny and Mary Fred did the cleaning inside and out. Then for the last two-thirds of the month, Mary Fred and Johnny would do the cooking together. "Because Beany knows more about balanced meals and cheap cuts than Johnny and I put together," Mary Fred told Ander.

Out in the lighted garage Ander worked with swift, careful hands wrapping steaming cloths on Mr. Chips' swollen foreleg. He stopped once and looked at Mary Fred thoughtfully. "I've always heard that phrase 'of the people, by the people, for the people,' but doggone if it ever made real sense until I sat there with you folks and saw that your family was a democracy with each one having a voice in it."

"Lots of voice," Mary Fred laughed.

Johnny called out to them from the back step, "Mary Fred, Miss Hewlitt says it'll be stupendous—the book, I mean."

That was on Friday night. Beany was up at six the next morning and, like a commanding general, routed out Johnny to shovel the snowy walks. She called Mary Fred, who an-

35

swered, "Okay, okay, I'll be right down," and dropped back into the warm drowsy depths from which she had been roused.

The door's opening wakened her and she groaned inwardly, "This is Beany coming to pull the covers off me." Sleepily she gripped the blanket's edge and burrowed deep under it and waited, braced. But no hand yanked at the covers. She opened one eye warily, then the other. A little girl with cheeks blue from the cold, with a great bushel basket, was down on all fours peering under the bed.

Mary Fred stretched luxuriously and said, "Hi there, Lorna! Did you lose something?"

The little five-year-old said, "The place is alive with them, Jock says."

"With what, cutie?"

"With rabbits, Jock says. He says I could fill a basket full without batting an eye, Jock says."

Mary Fred yawned herself out of bed. She disillusioned the little girl, "We've only got one rabbit, honey. But he's almost big enough to fill that basket."

Lorna and her brother Jock were two refugee children sent over from England to their great-uncle, a man who tended Miss Hewlitt's small acreage and who lived in a two-room cottage of his own close to the English Lit teacher's bungalow. Often on week ends the Malones had taken the two children into their home and tried to make up to them for the loneliness they couldn't help knowing with their half-sick old Uncle Charley and Miss Hewlitt, whose job kept her at school all day.

Miss Hewlitt was under Mary Fred's window talking to Johnny, whose snow shovel had ceased its scraping. As Mary

Fred went to her window to close it, she heard Johnny say, "I was thinking about the book in the night—thinking how we could have, for a pattern weaving through the book, the news items of the paper. You know, jumping through the years, and then fill in from them."

"Yes," said Miss Hewlitt, with the slow thoughtfulness of a mind visualizing it.

Mary Fred closed the window. Lorna was mourning. "I know about Frank—he's so big. I like little teeny-weeny rabbits."

Mary Fred sought to lift her disappointment as she squirmed into her faded red, third-best sweater. "Frank is a little on the big side, but he makes faces at you. Like this—" She gave a graphic demonstration, noting that Lorna did seem intrigued.

Miss Hewlitt was waiting at the foot of the stairs with the small, swaggering Jock, and she said to Mary Fred as she descended, "Mary Fred, I know it's imposing on you to ask you to keep the children for us today. But poor old Charley is just beside himself at times trying to keep up with these two. I promised to take them off his hands today, but I have some research at the library which will keep me all day."

From the kitchen came Lorna's happy trill, Jock's braggart Cockney accent, as they talked to Beany. "This will give the children something to talk about for days and days," Miss Hewlitt said.

"Of course we'll keep them, Miss Hewlitt."

Miss Hewlitt had brought a sack of bananas, some whipping cream, and another present which brought an almost audible groan from Beany—two dozen eggs. "And all those mangled eggs spilling out of our icebox now," whispered

Beany to Mary Fred as Miss Hewlitt went out the front door.

Lorna came running in from the back steps. "Frank did wiggle his nose, just like you did, Mary Fred."

5

The Hero of Harkness High

MONDAY morning dawned like any other day. Outside the sun tried to push through a wintry sky, while inside oatmeal bubbled and Mary Fred buttered toast with her French book propped open against the sugar bowl. Mary Fred had no way of knowing that it was to be a day of wondrous significance to her. She had no way of knowing, as she shoved her feet into her saddle shoes, that her feet would return from school treading, not on snowy sidewalks, but on rosy clouds.

She was so busy feeding Mr. Chips and wiping down the stairs and setting the rooms to rights that she had no more than a minute to run a comb through her hair and fasten her pompadour curl with two bobby pins. But that was the last time, for many a day, that caring for Mr. Chips, writing a hurried note to Elizabeth, and planning menus was to seem important. And the last time that she was to run a thoughtless comb through her dark, curly hair and feel satisfied with it.

The school day that Monday started out like almost any other day. Mary Fred, passing Lila's corner, was joined by her as she had been for some eleven years—Lila, with her friendly, adoring smile. Another three blocks and Janet McKean joined them—short, happy, crinkly-eyed, witty Janet, who wore shades of reddish brown to bring out the glint in her reddish-brown hair and the sparkle of her reddish-brown eyes. One of the wits at Harkness High had remarked that Janet McKean could laugh out loud with her eyes.

They always had to wait for Alberta, always had to grumble at her for being late. Alberta, with her blonde hair and pink-and-white skin and violet-blue eyes, was the prettiest of the four girls and she knew it, and her very conceit, which remained unruffled under all their ribbing, was refreshing. Alberta guided the talk toward the Spring Formal and the dress she was designing in Costume Designing. She had samples of taffeta and net and jersey which she dangled before them.

Alberta asked, "What's this fantastic story, Mary Fred, about you buying a horse with the money your grandmother sent you for a formal?"

"I just bought half of him with the fifteen dollars Nonna sent me for my birthday."

Janet McKean, who was interested in psychology, said, "Imagine a grandmother who insists on being called Nonna! The woman has a vanity complex."

"She's my step-grandmother," Mary Fred said. "And she just isn't the kind of a female you'd call Grandma."

Mary Fred had a mental picture of Nonna as they saw her on those fleeting stopover visits when she was hurrying from her successful interior-decorating business in Philadelphia to the Pacific coast. She was their mother's stepmother, and she had left Denver for Philadelphia about the time Mother had married. Nonna was slender and alert, and her hair, under her well-chosen hats, was a copper blonde. She looked thirtyish, but Beany, mathematician and realist, said, "She's closer to fifty. If our mother were alive, she'd be thirty-nine, and Nonna was about ten years older. I'll bet her hair is touched up."

At school the day began as usual except for a current of excitement that ran through the halls. "Did you know Dike Williams is back?" Dike Williams, a senior, was easily the school's biggest Big Shot. He was a football idol; sports writers gave him most of the credit for Harkness High's championship. Basketball was coming up, and he was the surest shot on the team. To add to his heroic aura, he had been hurt in the last game of the season in December and had been out of school until this day in January.

Today Dike Williams was back, and the very tempo of the school seemed quickened. No student was more quoted in the school paper than Dike Williams. In the latest issue there had been these columns: "My Favorite Food; My Favorite Amusement; My Favorite Girl." Mary Fred remembered, as did all Harkness High, Dike Williams' favorites—hamburgers; dancing; and as for the favorite girl, "I'll take a smooth little queen." He didn't add, but he might as well have, "No studes or mop-squeezers for me."

That was Harkness High jargon. The studes were the spectacled grinds with high grades. The mop-squeezers were the girls who served on committees, who worked on the paper, who did the grubby, behind-the-scene jobs. They were the ones who worked extra in Domestic Science to bake cookies for Senior Mother's Day. They drove out to the country the afternoon before the Hallowe'en party and brought back corn fodder and pumpkins to decorate the gym. They were the ones who got prices on doughnuts and cider, and at the party they stayed late to see that all the glasses got back to the lunchroom with no casualties.

The queens were the ones who, on Senior Mother's Day, dawdled through the halls with their mothers and munched the cookies. The queens danced every dance at the Hallowe'en party and didn't worry about leaving a glass on some shadowed window sill. The queens read, with an indulgent smile, the wisecracks in the school paper about themselves, which some hard-working mop-squeezer had thought up, working till twelve at night in the stuffy journalism room.

Mary Fred had been to innumerable rallies and victory dances where Dike Williams had been feted. Like ninety-nine per cent of the girls at Harkness, she placed him high on a pedestal. She had read of his preference for the queens of Harkness, and of the world, and she had not been surprised. Sylvia, the senior girl he dated oftenest, was every inch a queen. But, reading it, Mary Fred had known a twinge of regret that she belonged to the mop-squeezer class.

Today Dike Williams was back! He was wearing a bandage on his shoulder which showed under his open collar, and underclassmen said to each other, "J'see Dike's bandage?" It was almost a *croix de guerre*.

In the late afternoon Mary Fred was at her locker getting out her cooking apron, when Dike came up to her. "Hi, Dike!" she greeted him. She'd forgotten how widely magnetic his grin was, how widely straight his shoulders were. "Hi, sugar," he said, and added, "I call my honey sugar—because she's hard to get."

Mary Fred laughed. In another day that would be all

42

over the school. He fell into step beside her. "Well, aren't you glad to see me back? Or aren't you? You never came to see me all the time I was laid up. No wonder I ran a temp day after day."

Mary Fred caught her breath. That was faster work than she was used to. She wished she could think of a spicy comeback, but all she could manage was a ten-year-old's "Oh yeah?"

They climbed the stairs to the third floor. He left her at the big double doors of Cooking Lab. "This your last class?" he asked.

"Um-hmm."

"I'll be hangin' round."

Mary Fred's heart was thumping hard. But she mustn't be silly. Maybe Dike was mad at Sylvia—no, that wasn't it —he was just practicing his line on her. No, that wasn't it— he was just feeling fraternal his first day back at school. Of course, that was it! But Mary Fred had a hard time concentrating on all the teacher was telling them about the reason why eggs should be cooked at a low temperature. "There is no such thing as a hard-boiled egg," the teacher was saying earnestly. "It may be hard-cooked without boiling."

Mary Fred wouldn't let herself go hurrying out of class. Dike had forgotten, she was sure, that he had even said he'd be there. . . . But he was there, waiting for her.

She could feel the surprise of the other girls as he took her arm and went down the stairs with her to her locker. Lila came up as Mary Fred squirmed into her reversible, but she fell back in awed respect at sight of Dike Williams taking Mary Fred's books.

Down the thirty-two steps of Harkness High's front steps they swung in rhythm. He said, "I hear the French Club is having its shindig after school tomorrow aft."

"Yes—sort of an initiation of our new members. Ice cream'n everything."

"Will you be my squaw at the party?"

"Why—why—" But she had no breath to answer him.

"If I asked you on bended knee, would you?"

Her words came in a tumultuous rush, "Of course I would —of course! Oh, I'd love to!"

He stopped at the corner. "I wish I could walk home with you but I promised Coach I'd be at the gym." He lingered to say, "Your dad is Martie Malone of the *Call*, isn't he?" Mary Fred nodded. "I always read whatever he says on sports," Dike paid tribute. "He knows his rutabagas. Someone was telling me that he and Coach Hibbs up at State were buddies all through school."

"Oh yes, they were," Mary Fred said. "They still are. Coach Hibbs is like one of our family. He always comes to our house when he's in town."

"He does, eh? Gee—"

And then one of the fellows called to him, "Dike, hey guy, we're waiting for you!"

And that was when Mary Fred's saddle shoes never touched the icy pavements—they were treading rosy clouds while her heart kept thumping, "Dike Williams asked me to be his squaw at the French party. Dike Williams asked me." She couldn't believe it. Dike Williams, senior Big Shot; Dike Williams, who preferred queens, singling her out, Mary Fred Malone, unspotlighted junior *and* a mop-squeezer.

All that evening the things Mary Fred did were only movements of her hands and feet. What should she wear to the French party? At these school affairs one wanted to look nifty in a casual sort of way; never in a dressed-up way.

She stood in her closet and lifted each hanger out and inspected its burden with nervous, critical eyes. Her wardrobe had never seemed so skimpy, or so wretchedly chosen. Look at that blue dress with military brass buttons! That might look all right on Beany but certainly not on the girl Dike Williams was squawing. Oh, and that cream flannel with gaudy red embroidery on the pockets! She suddenly remembered Alberta saying once that embroidered pockets looked like a basement bargain. Alberta was right—*it did*. Well, here was her newest yellow sweater. She'd have to wash it. But it was her best bet, worn with her plaid skirt.

She glanced down at her plaid skirt and groaned inwardly. She had spilled acid on it in chemistry, and even by stretching her sweater in the direction of the jagged, match-sized burn, she couldn't cover it. She had caught it together but it had a pulled look. Oh, for Mrs. No-Complaint Adams to wheedle into patching it!

But there was no Mrs. Adams and she was to be Dike Williams' girl at the French party. So she hunted through drawers and window seat until she found the belt that had come with the skirt. She ripped it apart and set about matching the plaid and whipping down the edges of the burn in unlumpy fashion.

And, as she sat cross-legged on the window seat where she could see herself in the mirror over the dressing table, Mary Fred took unhappy stock of herself, too. Now there was Alberta with her flaxen hair and violet-blue eyes, who was the perfect pale-blond type; and there was Janet with her reddish-brown hair and reddish-brown eyes, who was, as she put it, a chocolate-brunette (Johnny called her the nut-brown maiden); then there was their own lovely Elizabeth, who was a warm-hued blonde. But what was she, Mary Fred? Just a tried-to-be-brunette. Father had said, "It's an old Irish custom to put gray eyes in brunettes with a dirty finger."

Mary Fred sighed in dissatisfaction at her dark, unruly hair always breaking away from the bondage of bobby pins. And her hands! Such scrubwoman, stableboy hands! She must take time to beautify them.

Uneasily she plunged the new lemon-yellow sweater into suds. Washing often did funny things to sweaters. She stretched it carefully over towels on the ironing board, then, in a frenzy of anxiety lest it mightn't be dry by morning, she transferred it to the radiator with a towel under it.

She was pressing the patch which she had hoped would be invisible but which wasn't, and Beany was just saying, "But you should have slanted the patch piece a little more," when Ander came over. He brought some liniment he had bought downtown. It was the same they used on the ranch for sore and swollen tendons.

Mary Fred went out to the garage with him. Funny that seeing how almost unlimping Mr. Chips was this evening wasn't a thrill. Funny that Ander had seemed so all right up till now. But this evening he seemed farmery. Her mind kept seeing Dike Williams' black hair with damp comb marks through it. Ander's hair seemed straw-colored by contrast.

That night Mary Fred put her hair up on wire curlers. It made uncomfortable sleeping. And in the middle of the night she worried for fear the radiator might make creases in the yellow sweater drying on it; she got up and went down to put an extra towel under the sweater.

The French Club initiation party was held in the gym. A classmate of Mary Fred's, Norbett Rhodes, was president of the club, and Mary Fred was the secretary. Norbett was a thin-faced, moody boy and the class laughed among themselves because he had no sooner been elected president than he had had stationery printed with his name on it and, under his name, *Président de l'Académie française*.

At the party Norbett clung close to Mary Fred. It was customary for the president and secretary to dance the first dance together. But when the first thump sounded on the piano Dike Williams came up and quite masterfully, yet casually, swept Mary Fred onto the floor. What were customs to royalty like Dike Williams? Mary Fred saw Norbett glowering after her. Let him glower. She was Dike Williams' girl.

The attitude of the whole school was different the next day. Seniors, who had hitherto passed Mary Fred by, spoke to her, "Hi, gal!" She moved in a glad haze. Lila, who had never had a date except one made by her mother—via the mother of the boy—was openly awed. "But you're pretty wonderful yourself, Mary Fred," she paid tribute. Alberta, who had always been condescending because her prettiness and her clothes claimed the spotlight, underwent a change. She deferred to Mary Fred now. Only Janet was skeptical in her crinkly-eyed teasing, "Aye, the lad has charm and athletic prowess, period."

At home, too, Mary Fred moved in roseate ecstasy. The very thump of the oiled mop kept time to the thump of her heart, "I'm Dike Williams' girl. Just imagine!"

Beany attacked the meal-getting like an energetic little gopher. And no fault could be found with her meals. Monday night, scalloped ham and potatoes with a fancy fruit salad which also served as dessert. Tuesday night, Swiss steak, baked squash, upside-down cake. Wednesday night Beany tried a new recipe, pigs in blankets, and it was so successful that Beany sat at her end of the table and preened herself. She took on a superior, advice-giving attitude toward Johnny and Mary Fred.

Her only fiasco was some oatmeal macaroons that went wrong, and Johnny lost no time in seizing upon one—though it must have started out to be two or three—which ran all over the cookie pan and did resemble a relief map of Africa. Johnny, hoping to put Beany in her place, mounted it on a board. He marked off the oceans, and the Cape of Good Hope, and hung it on the dining room wall.

Beany's eyes sparkled with a retaliatory glint. "Just you wait, Mr. Wise Man, just you wait till you have your turn."

"Okay, precious, okay," Johnny said expansively. "If we can go that relief map one better, you can put it on the wall for every passer-by to gaze upon."

A letter came from Elizabeth in California. "Don expects to leave any day, and I'm all packed, so that the minute he kisses me goodbye, I'll scamble onto the next train for home."

Saturday was Father's birthday. Beany spent the whole morning baking and icing and decorating a cake for him. But he telephoned toward noon to ask them to come down and have lunch with him at his Press Club. He found he would be tied up at the paper all evening and wouldn't get home for his birthday dinner.

It upset Beany, who had planned a dramatic entrance with candles lighted on her cake. And it upset Mary Fred because she had asked Dike Williams to come to the birthday dinner, and he had accepted eagerly. She telephoned him to tell him there would be no birthday dinner that evening. "There won't!" he repeated disappointedly. "Why, gal, that's what I call letting a fellow down hard. I broke another date to come."

"I'm sorry," Mary Fred said with troubled humility.

He said, "Well, maybe it isn't too late to horn in on this date I broke." He hung up the telephone without any friendly banter.

Mary Fred dressed to go down to her father's luncheon with an unnamed heaviness inside her. Dike hadn't even mentioned coming over and keeping the date with her, even though her father wouldn't have a birthday dinner.

6

Father Calls a Council

THE three Malones, Johnny, Beany, and Mary Fred, sat in the red leather chairs at the Press Club and waited for Father. Mary Fred saw him pushing through the wide glass doors. He looked tall, thin, and tired, with the wrinkles around his eyes and mouth finely drawn. He saw them and smiled, and all the tired lines took an upward turn.

Father ordered the luncheon. Always these luncheons at the Press Club, with everyone stopping to speak to Martie Malone and with him saying proudly, "Meet the young Malones," were times of happy festivity. Mary Fred looked at the well-scrubbed Beany, her straw-colored braids damply glistening, wearing the turquoise linen blouse under her Scotch plaid jumper, and squirming in delight. She looked at Johnny, who was in his element; Johnny belonged here among these men who wrote out thoughts on a typewriter.

Mary Fred herself felt oddly estranged, stranded between two worlds. Since Dike Williams had taken her up she had somehow edged out of all these things that had once mattered so much. And yet with the memory of Dike's hanging up swiftly, of his saying, "Well, maybe it isn't too late to horn in on this date I broke," she felt pushed out of that glad new world too.

Beany, still thinking of the cake on the sideboard at home with the pink icing spelling out "FATHER," asked, "Are you sure you can't come home for dinner?"

"No chance, Cabbage. The war news is pretty discouraging. I want to rewrite my whole editorial." He sighed heavily.

Beany said righteously, "You shouldn't work so much extra time. Other people don't."

Father said thoughtfully, "I'll tell you the kind of editorial I want this to be in tomorrow's paper. I want it to wake up everyone who reads it. I want them to feel shaken—shaken hard enough to stop thinking of their own comforts and conveniences. So they'll say to themselves, 'Yes, I'm tired and overworked and disappointed, but I'm better off than the boys in foxholes at Bataan or the sailors swimming through flaming oil.'"

They sat very silent.

And then he said, "I called you all down here for more than a luncheon—it's a Malone council table. I've something I want to talk over with you. The paper wants me to hop over to Hawaii and take the place of our war correspondent for a few months; he was hurt during the attack. I wanted to talk it over with you all."

Out of their stunned soberness, Mary Fred managed to ask thinly, "Do you want to go?"

His quizzical smile seemed to reach through her cold numbness and warm her heart a little. "I'd rather stay home and argue with you kids, and have old Red sleeping on my foot in the evenings. But it's like going into service; you can't think of what you'd like, or what you wouldn't. I'd be doing my bit by going over there. Do you Malones think you could manage awhile without any parent at all?"

They looked bleakly at each other. It was incentive to get up in the morning to know that Father would be grinning at them across the breakfast table and yelling, "Bring me my oats—and a stack of wheats." How Mrs. Adams had loved to hear him yell that! And the day always had a lift at the end because of Father's coming home.

Beany was the first to speak around a piece of muffin and a lump in her throat, "I think you ought to go." And Johnny added with forced cheer, "Sure, you know us—the Malones can always make out." Mary Fred said, "And Elizabeth will be home any day now. A house is never lonesome with Elizabeth in it."

They discussed it while they waited for the ice cream. Father had already telephoned Mrs. No-Complaint Adams and she had agreed to stay nights with them, sleeping in her old room in the basement, but hurrying back in the mornings to her daughter's home. "I wish we had a nice old grandmother to come in and mother you chicks," Father said. "But the only near-grandmother in our family is a very efficient interior decorator."

"That we wouldn't dare call Grandma," put in Beany.

"She said in her last letter that she was going to sell out and would come for a long visit," Johnny said.

"She's always going to sell," Father said. "She's always going to come and see how you 'poor children' are getting along. But she'd be lost if she didn't have a half-dozen people to order around."

"How soon will you go?" Mary Fred asked.

"In about ten days."

"How long will you be gone?"

"Well—say two months. It might be longer—it might possibly be less."

Their desolation was momentarily lifted by the head waiter coming toward their table wearing a wide grin and bearing a birthday cake with lighted candles. And a chorus of men's voices from all parts of the room took up the chant, "Happy birthday, dear Martie—happy birthday to you." They laughed uproariously at his look of surprise.

At that moment Mary Fred forgot Dike Williams entirely and knew only a great rush of sobering pride that Martie Malone was her father. For as he sat there, smiling through his tiredness, she felt his greatness from his very graciousness. Mrs. Adams had said it, "—you'd never find anyone so good and so smart as Martie Malone." Mary Fred thought for one awful minute she was going to cry. She was thankful when Johnny, the awkward, knocked her purse on the floor and she could busy herself picking it up.

The birthday cake was feather-light, velvety of texture. Johnny was hearty both in eating and in praising it. "It ought to be good," Beany said viciously. "I'll bet it takes about fifteen egg whites."

As it happened, she had guessed exactly right. For the chef came out from the kitchen to accept their thanks and Johnny's wholehearted praise. "Thees cake," he beamed, "I make eet up myself how to make. In eet I put fifteen egg whites, light like clouds. Eet ees call Lady Eleanor cake after our First Lady. No one knows my recipe—" with an appreciative wink at Johnny, "only to a very good friend I would geeve it to."

Beany's ten-day reign in the kitchen expired, if not in a

blaze of glory, at least in a haze of nice satisfaction. It ended on Monday night and Mary Fred and Johnny were to take over on Tuesday morning.

Beany had used exactly one-third of the housekeeping money. Father had left the control of the hundred dollars, which was to pay for the housekeeping and the groceries, entirely to the three managers. Because Beany was all taut desire to get the yellow-plaid gingham and all anxiety for fear the bolt would be sold out or raised in price, they let her take her share in advance and buy the required yardage of sun-catcher.

And then of course there was Mr. Chips! His grain and alfalfa couldn't wait till the end of the month when Mary Fred should have earned her share of the housekeeping fund. She had to draw on her share too.

So did Johnny. Not only did the red car demand a battery recharge, but Johnny's old typewriter typed with pale illegibility for want of a new ribbon. Johnny and Emerson had started The Book. It was hard to say who prodded-on whom. But Mary Fred dropped off to sleep many nights to the music of those rattly keys under Johnny's fevered pounding.

Mrs. Thompson, the egg woman from Ander's ranch, stopped to report on the fixing of the fender and light. She had had it fixed in their own Wyoming town and she brought the bill, sixteen dollars plus thirty-two cents tax. Johnny paid her some on it and promised to pay the rest as he got it.

On a cold Tuesday morning Johnny and Mary Fred took over the feeding of the Malones. It was torture for Mary Fred, the sleepyhead, to obey the alarm clock and scamper through the gray chill to the kitchen to light the broiler and put on water for cereal. Martie Malone insisted on having a breakfast heartening enough to stay by him in case he got too busy to go out for lunch.

Mary Fred and Johnny got a daring idea. Why couldn't they plan menus around the eggs they had and thus pare the food budget? For Mary Fred just had to have a new pleated skirt. That one she was wearing with her inexpert patch! She tried to remember and hold her books over it, but she couldn't always remember. Ordinarily it wouldn't matter but now she was Dike Williams' girl. Forty dollars seemed more than adequate to buy food for twenty days. Surely she could squeeze out a few dollars for a pleated skirt.

But Mary Fred found that skirts were more expensive than when she had last bought one. "Everything woolen has gone up," the clerk said suavely. Five dollars and ninety-five cents was more than she had planned to pay, but this one was a love—pleats in front and back, and with shades of gray and green and enough yellow to go with her best yellow sweater that Dike liked. Alberta, the fashion expert, often told Mary Fred that with her gray eyes and high coloring she ought to wear grays and greens. Looking at her reflection in the store mirror, she saw herself walking down Harkness' halls beside Dike in this perky skirt. . . . She bought it and a pair of yellow shorties to wear with her saddle shoes.

She and Johnny thumbed through cookbooks for egg recipes. Cream puffs, scrambled eggs, Spanish omelet. Johnny cooked better, even as he wrote better, when something inspired him. One day he stopped at a vegetable stand to buy celery and the Italian owner told him of a dish which was, "Pretty swell, by gollee!"

55

Johnny worked with deft absorption, boiling some of his uncracked eggs. He took out the yolks and mashed them and seasoned them with finely cut, sautéed mushrooms and parsley and cream. The stuffed eggs were covered in a casserole with creamed mushrooms and baked with buttered crumbs, and a last sprinkling of mashed, hard-cooked egg yolks on top to add a crisp, crunchy brownness.

Father had brought home as guest that night for dinner a newspaper woman from Brazil. Her first name was Raphaela and her last name too unpronounceable for the Malones. She went into ecstasies over Johnny's "Italian Eggs Supreme." "I am enraptured—I am bewitched by these so divine eggs."

Johnny strutted importantly. "You see," he said to Beany, "you mean well, but it's imagination that gives the magic touch to cooking. It's that old creative instinct in the cook that makes the difference between eating and dining."

And Beany could say nothing. *But look out, Johnny, my boy*, Mary Fred thought. *Look out that Beany doesn't get anything on you.*

Day after day went by and still no word came from Elizabeth. It had been over a week now since her letter had arrived, saying she would be there any day. But even Elizabeth's coming that had once seemed so all-important to Mary Fred was only dim background for her own great happiness now.

Every evening Dike Williams walked home from school with her. He did such unexpected things. "What are you doing tonight, Mary Fred?"

"Going to the opera at the auditorium."

"Who with?"

"Johnny and Carlton. It's the spring opera the Cathedral

56

always puts on. *Aida!* And Johnny and his pal Carlton are soldiers in the second act, and I wanted to see them."

"On Annie Oakleys?"

"No. No Annie Oakleys when it's for sweet charity."

"Your father going?"

"He doesn't know for sure. He wants to run over and see it with us if he can possibly get away from the *Call.*"

"Why can't you go with me?" Dike asked.

"I can," she said happily. "I'd lots rather go with you than with Johnny and Carl."

At the auditorium Mary Fred and Dike waited in the lobby, watching for Martie Malone. But evidently he was too busy to leave the editorial room. When at last Dike went to buy tickets, the house was sold out except the gallery. He came back to Mary Fred mumbling, "You don't catch me climbing clear up to the peanut gallery. You wait here."

Something the alert, succinct Janet McKean had said wriggled into Mary Fred's mind while she waited: "Dike Williams is the poor hero with the tastes of a capitalist's son."

Dike was talking to the head usher. The head usher called the manager, and then an usher led them around the side aisle and into a box. Dike leaned over and whispered as he helped Mary Fred squirm out of her coat, "Slick, I calls it. This is the governor's box. I happened to know he was called out of town this afternoon, so I told the manager that he telephoned me and told me to use his seats."

Mary Fred gasped. "Oh—but I don't think you should!"

He laughed. "Listen, Snooks, it's what you get that counts, not how you get it."

The curtain went up then and Mary Fred forgot what he said. But later those words were to leap out at her from her own hurt and humiliation.

57

7

Elizabeth Comes Home

EVERY day the Malones said to each other, "Surely we'll
hear from Elizabeth today"; or perhaps, "Maybe Elizabeth
will come today!"

Some afternoons the telephone would be ringing when
Mary Fred walked in the front door from school, and it
would be Father, whose first query was always, "Heard anything from Elizabeth?"

And Mary Fred would hurriedly shuffle through the
letters she had just taken out of the mailbox and answer
regretfully, "No, not a thing, Father."

Elizabeth's bed, and half the closet, were ready and waiting. Elizabeth would share the suite of two rooms with
Mary Fred. Only Elizabeth, not being the ardent fresh-air
fan Mary Fred was, would sleep in the big room with the
fireplace, while Mary Fred slept out on the glassed-in porch
which was really a room.

On this February day when Mary Fred and Dike Williams sauntered home from school the sun was out in earnest,

giving false promise of spring. Mary Fred's mind told her she should not loiter. There was work to do at home. But her heart slowed her feet because it was happiness to walk with Dike. Dike and his wisecracks! Then the next day in the hall between classes, in Foods, or in English Lit, Mary Fred would requote him to an admiring and envious audience.

They were turning in at her gate when Beany opened the door and called, "Hurry in, Mary Fred. Elizabeth's down at the station. She telephoned and Johnny and Ander went down. Ander went so he could drive."

Dike said, as he came in with Mary Fred, "Elizabeth is the one they still talk about at school, eh what? Glamour, beauty, and what it takes?"

"Wait till you see her," Mary Fred said. "She was freshman escort for the Varsity queen at Homecoming, and she was one of the Maypole dancers, and even news photographers, who get fed up with taking bridal pictures, said she was a treat for the cameras." Mary Fred wanted to sprinkle all the stardust she could on Elizabeth, as though her sister's charm might somehow enhance herself in Dike's eyes. "Look, here's a picture of her in her going-away clothes."

"Pretty hair," Dike said.

"Beany says that whenever she reads about someone's hair being an aureole about her face, she thinks of Elizabeth."

Together they gazed upon the picture of a slim, lovely, eighteen-year-old bride. The frilly ruffle around her neck fell outside and emphasized the dark, snug-fitting suit. A picture hat sat back and framed the glow of hair and the young radiance of her face.

Beany yelled out, "I thought I heard a car. Yessir, here they are now!"

The red car was already drawn up at the doorway. Ander had leaped out and was helping his passenger to alight. Mary Fred started out the door, then stopped in amazement.

That couldn't be Elizabeth! The late afternoon sun was heartless in accentuating the wanness, the rumpledness of the girl. Even her shoes looked scuffed and dusty. That couldn't be Elizabeth's dark blue, going-away suit—that linty, wrinkled thing with a bedraggled frill half under the coat, half out! And where was the glinting aureole of hair? Under a taffeta hat that had lost all tilt, her light hair fell in limp disorder.

Elizabeth took a shaky step. And then Ander, quite easily and casually, lifted her up in his arms and carried her up the porch steps and into the front room. Mary Fred afterward remembered guiltily that, for the first minute, she was ashamed of Elizabeth's making such a poor entry after she, Mary Fred, had bragged so inordinately to Dike Williams about her loveliness and her chic.

Elizabeth smiled shakily. "I was—delayed. I've been over two weeks coming. Our train had to sidetrack to let troop trains go by—and that's when I knew I—I couldn't make it. I've been at a little dinky town in Wyoming—you could hear the coyotes yell like everything every night."

Beany yelled suddenly, "Johnny, Johnny, you're dragging the shawl!" Mary Fred looked out to see Johnny coming up the steps carrying a bundle wrapped in a pale pink shawl. He stumbled once over the fringe of shawl and almost fell, before Beany could grab it up and tuck it in. "It's a boy," Johnny made proud announcement on the threshold.

Something big and choking rose in Mary Fred's chest.

60

"Oh, Elizabeth—" was all she could manage as she put her arms around her sister.

"My goodness, you've got him upside down," Beany said, peering under the layer of blankets. Mary Fred said, "Here, let me take him." She lifted the shawl and looked into a red, wrinkled face which was puckering into a wail, and instinctively she crooned, "There, there, little fellow—don't cry." His small hands felt like cold, moist flower petals.

Beany and Ander were taking charge of Elizabeth. Dike Williams, for all his football prowess, stood about, helpless. It was Ander who showed Johnny how they must make a saddle of their hands and carry Elizabeth up the stairs. "The baby's just two weeks old. The doctor at this little hospital in Wyoming told me not to climb stairs yet," Elizabeth's pale lips said.

Her teeth were chattering weakly and Ander said, "You're getting right to bed."

Beany scurried up ahead of Johnny and Ander and their burden. She pulled down the bedclothes. She rummaged through Elizabeth's suitcase for her bedroom slippers and pajamas and housecoat.

Mary Fred jiggled the fussing baby in her arms. She wanted suddenly to sit in front of a fire and warm the baby's cold feet and hands and fold him into a dry diaper. She wished Dike would offer to get wood and coal and make a fire in the bedroom fireplace. But somehow you didn't ask the mighty Dike Williams to do things.

Beany called down, "Mary Fred, fix a hot-water bottle for Elizabeth."

Mary Fred was in the kitchen filling the hot-water bottle when the telephone rang. She answered it and let out a glad cry, "Oh, it's Father!"

He said, "Mary Fred, I'm calling from the airport. I ran out home this afternoon and packed my grip. They want me to get to Hawaii as soon as I can. To connect with the plane at Frisco, I have to catch this five-o'clock plane. Heard from Elizabeth?"

"She's here. She just came a few minutes ago. And guess what? She's got—"

Johnny was yelling down the stairs, "Hush! Hush! Elizabeth said for you not to tell him."

Mary Fred checked her words. Of course Elizabeth would want to tell him herself. Father said, "Let me talk to her."

They stretched the upstairs extension cord as far as they could into the bedroom, and then Ander motioned to Dike to help him pull the bed the few extra feet toward it, enabling Elizabeth to talk without getting up.

Mary Fred listened brazenly on the downstairs extension so she would not miss Father's joy when he was told of the baby. "Elizabeth—my dear, own Elizabeth," he said. "Are you all right, beloved?"

"Of course I am. Right as rain."

"Have you got everything you want? Have you got enough money?"

"Sir, what are you insinuating? Aren't I an officer's wife?"

"So you are, so you are! But just one thing more, does the officer's wife still love old Martie Malone?"

Mary Fred heard the choke in Elizabeth's voice, "Better than tongue can tell." That was a childhood joke between them.

But Martie Malone had evidently heard her voice break, too, for he said, "Look, my only, I'm going to take a later plane. I've got to see you with my own eyes."

62

The choke went out of Elizabeth's voice. "No, Martie Malone, you'll do no such thing," she said firmly. "You'll make sure you catch your plane. They need you over there in Hawaii. And don't you dare worry about me. I'll be here when you get back."

"Goodbye, then, Elizabeth. I'm glad you're safe at home. I've been uneasy about you. Tell the others goodbye for me. I'll write you all from Frisco. Be happy, won't you?"

Mary Fred replaced the telephone in its cradle with sober hands. Dike Williams said, "I guess your father will come right on home to see Elizabeth, won't he?"

"No, he's flying to Frisco right away. Elizabeth didn't tell him that her baby was born on her way home for fear he would worry about her. And he would have—he'd have worried himself sick."

Dike Williams said, "So he's not coming home! I thought sure I'd see him before he left." He mumbled something then about having to hurry on home.

Through all the upsetting confusion Mary Fred felt the disappointment in his voice—more than that—almost resentment. She was trying to understand it as the front door slammed behind him.

And then Beany roused her by calling down the stairs, "Mary Fred—oh, Mary Fred, come quick! Elizabeth's fainted!"

It seemed to the anxious watchers that Elizabeth's blue eyes were a long time flickering open. They could hear the baby fretting down on the couch in the living room all the time they worked with Elizabeth, holding smelling salts to her nose, rubbing her cold, thin hands. And when she could swallow, Mary Fred diluted brandy with hot water and held it to her lips.

"Elizabeth," reproached Beany worriedly, "whatever made you faint?"

"I haven't eaten anything all day," she apologized. "I left the hospital early this morning."

"Oughtn't you to have stayed there longer?" Johnny asked.

"I couldn't—I didn't have enough money. Don and I saved so hard for this, and we figured it all out, only we planned that I'd be here where I'd know the doctor and wouldn't have to pay him all at once. And so I'm broke. A soldier offered me some of his lunch but he looked so big— and hungry—"

Johnny got to his feet in such haste he stumbled over the suitcase. "Eggs are good for nursing mothers, aren't they?" he asked. And he was down the stairs two at a time.

At the same time Ander said he'd get wood for a fire and hurried out. Beany went down to get the crying baby. Elizabeth tried to turn her head away but Mary Fred saw the tears streaming down her pale cheeks. "Elizabeth, what's the matter?"

"Nothing, honey—nothing at all—now." Elizabeth reached for Mary Fred's hand, laughed thickly. "I'm like that old story of the little boy that had a bad time of it away from home but waited till he got home to cry. I didn't know how much I wanted some of my own around me—until I got here. I—I was pretty scared up there in that little town. And the way the wind did blow!"

"You should have telegraphed us."

"No," she said slowly, "it wouldn't have been right to worry you. I gave the hospital the wrong address so if they notified you of the birth you wouldn't be upset. Father wrote me that he had this important trip pending. Don and I talked everything over so often. In times like these, we agreed, everyone had his own burden, and no one else should add his. Don has his; Father has his; and this was mine."

"You're so brave, Elizabeth."

"No, I'm not. You'll never know how scared and lonely —just panicky—I was up there. But now I'm glad I faced it myself."

Mary Fred said softly, "I read some place where courage is fear that has said its prayers."

Elizabeth smiled tiredly as she wiped the tears away with a flinging of her arm across her face. "I said mine. But I found out kind folks are—everywhere. And I found out that I can take what anyone else can; and that's nice to know."

Ander came in with the wood. He hunkered down before the fireplace, wadded up newspapers. There was the heartening crackle of flame, the nice smell of wood smoke.

And here came Johnny balancing a tray on one hand. "A rush order of poached eggs on toast," he announced.

"Eggs," Elizabeth said delightedly, while all the rest looked at each other and laughed. "I'm so glad to have eggs. There seemed to be a shortage of them up in Wyoming."

"That's because the Wyoming people bring them to Denver," Ander said. He counseled Mary Fred from the doorway, "You watch the fire. I have to go now. Soon as it burns up good, put on this big lump of coal, and it'll last all evening. You let me know, Elizabeth, if you want anything else." He took a final peek at the baby before he left.

The baby was insisting upon attention. Elizabeth said, "All his clothes are in the black suitcase, Beany."

Beany tugged the suitcase into the middle of the floor, dropped on her knees to open it. She cried out, "My gosh, what are these? I wish you'd look!"

They all looked. The suitcase was full of khaki shirts, heavy socks, a few new handkerchiefs still in their cellophane wrappings, some writing paper, some more khaki shirts, and a pair of the biggest shoes they had ever seen.

Mary Fred said, "Land of love, Elizabeth, you must have got some soldier's suitcase and he got yours by mistake!"

Elizabeth said incredulously, "Oh, but I picked out my bulgy black one." She raised up on her arm and stared at the strange contents. "Yes, I must have," she admitted in a stricken voice. "The train was full of soldiers and the baggage got all mixed up. And this poor little sparrow with not a dry stitch to put on him."

Johnny said, "A fellow's got to have clothes," and ducked out swiftly.

Mary Fred wished ardently for Mrs. No-Complaint Adams; she would know what shift to do for a baby crying in discomfort with no change of diapers. Elizabeth was saying, "There must be some old soft sheets in the linen closet. And maybe a blanket that we could cut in two for extra blankets for him."

Mary Fred warmed the baby in front of the fire as she took off his wet clothes. She made him dry and warm and then laid him beside Elizabeth. In a half-hour all was beautiful, quiet peace. Beany and Mary Fred tiptoed about the work in the house. In a room dim with dusk and lighted only by the grate fire which warmed it, Elizabeth slept and her baby nursed at her breast and then slept beside her.

Strange, Mary Fred thought, as she peeked in at them, how we learn lines of poems and they're only lines of poems until sometimes they come whispering out of our own heart; like this line, "God's in his heaven, all's right with the world."

66

Just then Johnny came bursting in the front door and up the stairs. He was carrying a bundle, fully as large as a two weeks' bundle of laundry. He said, "I put an ad in the *Call*, 'If soldier finds he has suitcase of clothes that seem too small, please exchange.' And then I ran down to a little store on Broadway and bought a few things for the little fellow to last until we get the suitcase back."

Beany's and Mary Fred's eyes met. As though Johnny could buy a few of anything!

"I could only get six nightgowns," he apologized. "That was all the little store had. The clerk said not to get them too small, so I got the kind he can grow into."

Elizabeth held up a white outing-flannel gown bound in pink ribbon. Mary Fred snickered. It would easily fit a baby who could walk. But Elizabeth said happily, "Oh, Johnny, you love!"

"I got the diaper stuff cheaper by getting a bolt," Johnny said. "And then I thought I'd better get a few blankets. Look, this one has rabbits on it."

"Rabbits," groaned Beany. "Why do people always poke rabbits at children when they're too young to defend themselves?"

"They're beautiful blankets," Elizabeth insisted.

The minute they reached the foot of the stairs and were out of hearing of Elizabeth, Beany, the practical, demanded, "How much of the grocery money have you got left, Johnny?"

Mary Fred tried to defend him. "We've already cooked a week—no, eight days out of it—and we've spent fifteen dollars."

"That would leave twenty-five," said Beany.

"And then I bought that skirt—because, you know,

Johnny and I figured that if we used eggs we could save enough on the food budget. It was a little over six, counting tax."

"And you bought shorties, too," Beany pinned her down. "How much were they?"

"Thirty-nine cents," admitted Mary Fred guiltily.

"How much grocery money you got left now, Johnny?" Beany asked.

Johnny dug out of his pocket a five-dollar bill, a silver dollar, and some change. Mary Fred had to groan as she said, "Twelve days yet to go. And Elizabeth will need chops and cream soups and things like that."

Beany said, "You'd better put a pot of beans to soak. They're cheap."

"Sure," Johnny said, "and we can have beans as is, bean soup, baked beans, chile. We can eat beans and get chops for Elizabeth. And don't forget there are always eggs."

"Who could?" grunted Beany.

The next day Beany was up a good hour before her schedule called for. Long before Mary Fred and Johnny started getting breakfast and fixing lunches, Beany was cleaning the house, doing the extra jobs she usually left for after school. "I'll be late getting home this evening," she announced.

"Festivity at school?"

"No," shortly. "It's business."

She was late returning. Elizabeth was sitting up in the big rocker before the fire in her room. Mary Fred and Johnny had decided it would be more fun to carry all their suppers upstairs and eat with her. Beany came in just when Johnny was carrying up the tray of dishes and Mary Fred was following with the pot of cocoa and plate of cinnamon toast; Elizabeth had always loved cinnamon toast.

Beany motioned to Mary Fred to back down the stairs a step or two and she whispered to her impressively, "It's all right. I saw a lot of them that look worse than he does —and they haven't even his personality."

"Whose personality? What are you talking about?"

"Elizabeth's baby. I guess Elizabeth didn't notice it— but oh, it worried me, he was so wrinkled and old-looking."

"Why, Beany, you just compared him to pictures of babies in magazine ads and holy pictures. You've never seen as new a baby as our little fellow—the little mister, as Mrs. No-Complaint Adams called him last night."

"I've seen them just as new now," Beany said. "And the brand-new ones look old. It seems strange that they come so very old, and then they have to grow young before they can start growing old again."

"Where in the world have you been, Beany?"

"To St. Joseph's Hospital to look at their babies. I looked at them all, studied them. And our baby's beautiful." She giggled in remembrance. "I saw one over there that looked a lot like old Emerson Worth—I mean so sort of wise and disgusted. I just expected to hear it say, 'What wilt thou?' quoth God. 'Take it and pay for it.' "

"Did you go clear over to St. Joseph's just to see if other babies were as wrinkled and red as our little mister?"

Beany returned with dignity, "I went over to find out about the care of babies."

From that day on Beany was the authority. "The nurse at St. Joseph's said to hold him this way over the shoulder after he's nursed to expel any air he sucks in." . . . "The nurse at St. Joseph's said you could soon train them to sleep the night through."

69

The days grew cold again and slippery underfoot. Mary Fred was afraid to exercise Mr. Chips for fear he'd slip and undo all that she and Ander had gained by rubbing on liniment and applying hot packs. But Ander, who was a skilled horseman, took him out, scoffing all the while about the postage-stamp saddle.

"I know, I know," Mary Fred would retaliate, "you want a western saddle, big as a cruising vessel." Mary Fred accused him of alienating Mr. Chips' affection because now the black horse knew Ander's step and nickered happily when he heard it.

Saturday was, as Johnny said, Labor Day for the Malones. They did the washing on Saturday; and this Saturday, with the additions from Elizabeth and the baby, the clotheslines couldn't accommodate all the clothes.

About midmorning Miss Hewlitt's small car stopped in the driveway. Before Miss Hewlitt could reach the front step, Jock and Lorna were pushing in the door. Miss Hewlitt said, "Mary Fred, I meant to ask you first if it would be convenient for you to keep the scalawags today. I promised old Charley to take care of them while he went down to the Clinic, and now I have been called down to the Administration Building."

"Of course we'll keep them. Jock can take his turn at the wringer with Johnny. And all we have to do is put Frank in the basement and Lorna will be playing hide-and-seek with him all day—only Frank does the hiding."

What with the wringer, the rabbit named Frank, and the new baby upstairs that cried without being squeezed, Lorna and Jock were happy. And they liked the stairs. Neither Charley's two-room cottage nor Miss Hewlitt's bungalow had stairs. They found innumerable ways to descend without walking; they went thumping down in a sitting position, they went down head first, feet first.

Mary Fred carried up to Elizabeth an armful of baby clothes, watched Elizabeth's loving hands shake them and fold them. There was an extra loud thumping noise on the stairs and Mary Fred said, "I hope these youngsters won't bother you."

Elizabeth looked down at her own sleeping baby. "Let's do all we can for them," she said. "I keep thinking of my own little tyke and how if I had to be separated from him— Let's don't think of how much noise and trouble they are. I'd like to do for them—and for any other children—" The very gesture of her arms said, "Let's do for all the homeless children in the world."

The telephone rang. It was Dike Williams, and Mary Fred's heart leaped high. "Look," he said, "you're going to a basketball game with me this afternoon in case you don't know it."

"A basketball game?" she repeated.

"A college game," he said. "Coach Hibbs from State will be there scouting to see what these teams have got. I want you to go with me—you know him, don't you?—and I'd like to have you introduce me so I could—could talk to him."

She said feebly, "Oh, Dike, I'd just adore to—honest I would—but I can't."

"You can't! Why can't you?"

"It's a long, long story—a sad, sad story—a story that will make you cry." She meant her voice to be flippant as she quoted the song, but it wasn't. For suddenly the clothes flapping on the line, the clothes in the basement still to be starched, and all those blouses of Beany's to be ironed, and Jock and Lorna to be looked after, and the chili to be made for supper—all seemed the longest, saddest story she had ever heard—and a story that made her want to cry.

"You sure you can't kick over everything and come?"

"I just can't, Dike."

On that he hung up. And Mary Fred was filled with resentment at life—at Mr. Chips who had to be paid for by her own labor. She longed with heartsick longing for freedom from it. She wanted a closetful of clothes. She wanted to set forth happily with Dike Williams whenever he called and asked her.

8

The Spring Formal Grows Formidable

MONDAY all talk at Harkness High was of the big Spring Formal. Now that it was the next event on the school calendar all interest was focused on it. "Who you going with?" "What you going to wear?" Mary Fred was suddenly and unhappily brought face to face with the PROM. The first question no one asked her. Everyone supposed she was going with Dike Williams.

But Dike Williams hadn't given her a bid. Oh, but surely he would! Maybe he took it for granted that she knew he'd take her. She couldn't come right out and say, "Are you taking me to the Spring Formal?" All the week before, she had talked around it as much as she dared. "I'm on the committee for the Spring Formal. We decided on programs in the shape of tulips." He didn't answer that, and she went on, "Some of the committee want to serve ices in the shape of flowers."

"I'll take forget-me-not," he grinned, and then began to talk of basketball.

73

She envied Alberta and Janet and Lila, not their escorts, but their security in having them cinched. Alberta was going with one of the boys on the football team—not a Big Shot like Dike Williams, of course. The boy Janet McKean had skated with all winter had asked her. Lila was going with the most bashful junior at Harkness, by name of Fred Ellanger. But Fred's mother and Lila's mother were friends. " 'Nuff said," Lila muttered with a ragged little grin.

And Alberta's ivory lace dress was the pride of the sewing teacher. It was now on a dress form for all the class to admire while the teacher and Alberta decided whether the huge flat bow on the underskirt, which would show through the filmy lace, should be orchid color or perhaps silver.

"Have you got your formal yet?" Alberta asked Mary Fred.

Mary Fred answered sharply, "Don't you remember? My formal is black with a lame foreleg and a splash of white in his forehead. Fallen star, you might say."

At home, Elizabeth, sensing Mary Fred's uneasiness over the dance and thinking it was because of a dress, or rather the lack of one, put the question gently. "Mary Fred honey, are you worrying because you haven't a formal? Why can't you wear that dress I wore in the Maypole dance last year? I wore it to one of the army dances and everyone told me how pretty it was. And that blue will make your eyes lovely."

Elizabeth was reaching it out of the garment bag in the closet as she talked. She tried it on Mary Fred. The dress was of pale blue chiffon with a shower of rose petals appliquéd on the full skirt. "It won't be hard to shorten," Elizabeth said.

74

In front of the mirror Mary Fred stared into her own uneasy eyes—made more blue than gray by the dress. Of course, everyone would know this was Elizabeth's Maypole dress, because the dancers wore almost these same full-skirted, basque dresses every year. In one way it was a relief to know she had a dress, but in another it only sharpened her other worry. Supposing they went through all the motions of getting the dress shortened and freshened and then Dike didn't ask her. After all, Sylvia, the senior girl he used to date and still talked to in the halls, was the queen; Sylvia was smooth to dance with; Sylvia had that certain something.

She'd think this one minute, and then when Dike was all intimate attention, she'd say to herself, "Why, he intends to take me. Of course he does." She would remember the time he had asked her on such short notice to go to the opera at the auditorium, and that busy Saturday when he had telephoned her at noon about the basketball game in the afternoon. But if she only knew!

So on this Monday morning between classes it was with uneasy qualms that she joined in the talk of dresses, and what corsage she hoped she'd get. "Oh, Dike Williams will send an orchid," Alberta predicted.

"He won't pay for it," Janet said realistically, "but Dike's girl will flaunt an orchid."

Lila, who always defended anyone who was being attacked even by insinuation, said, "But that's all right, Janet. He's so popular. They were talking in chem one day about how stores and firms give him things because it's worth something just for him to wear it and say where he got it. The sporting-goods house gave him his sweater—"

Janet finished, "Because it was an ad for them to have it

75

over Dike's jaunty shoulders. And the jeweler gave him his class ring because he swung the class into getting them all at this certain jeweler's."

Mary Fred only listened uneasily. All the school knew it —that Dike came from a poor family, but that he wanted for nothing. Mary Fred squirmed to think of how her father would classify such practices. "Mooching by any other name is just as snide," he'd say.

Lila was still defending, "Dike pays his way by his own popularity—"

But Janet was firm, "He capitalizes his popularity and if you ask me, he's paying a high price for sweaters, sport shoes, class rings, leather notebooks, and theatre tickets, when he pays for them with his own self-respect."

"Oh hush, Janet," Alberta said, taking out her mirror to study her lipstick job. "Everyone's wild about Dike. You know you'd fall in a huddle if he looked at you. You'd rather go to the Prom with him than—"

Mary Fred ducked on to class. Supposing Alberta said right out, "Everyone envies Mary Fred because she's going with him."

Monday noon came, but although Mary Fred passed Dike in the lunchroom eating his favorite hamburger and he called to her, "How's my squaw?" he never mentioned Spring Formal. The whole basketball team had been out of town over the week end. If only he'd stop thinking basketball long enough to think prom.

On Monday afternoon as Mary Fred turned away from her locker someone was waiting for her. Her heart jumped a beat until she saw that it was not Dike Williams. It was Norbett Rhodes, president of *l'Académie française*.

He stopped her and asked bluntly, "How about going to the Spring Formal with me?" It was more of a challenge than an invitation, as though he meant, "I dare you to turn me down."

She said coolly, "Sorry. It can't be did."

"Why can't it?"

"Because I happen to have a date."

"You going with Dike Williams?" he challenged again.

She wished with all her heart that she could say, "Yes, I'm going with Dike Williams." But she couldn't. So she evaded the question with a curt, "What do you think?"

"What do I think?" he answered with a mean laugh. "I'll tell you what I think. I think you're in for the hardest fall you ever got. Do I get a laugh out of you thinking Dike Williams is nuts about you, when all the time he's only making a play for getting subsidized next year at State U!"

Mary Fred's voice shook with anger. "I don't see how Dike Williams' plans for next year have anything to do with the Spring Formal one way or the other."

She started to pass him but he caught her by the arm. "Oh, you don't! Well, then, you're the only one in all Harkness who doesn't! Didn't it ever occur to you that he wants to get on the good side of Martie Malone so he'll have Coach Hibbs give him one of the fattest plums up at State? In case you don't know, it's called subsidizing and it makes a lot of difference to football players who want to go on to college. Dike Williams is one of these poor but ambitious boys. But he couldn't take one of the messy jobs—like washing dishes. Not the mighty Dike Williams. No, he's out to get something soft."

77

His words were like a blow, but she wouldn't let him see her flinch. "They teach us in Foods that mean dispositions are caused by a deficiency in diet," she said coolly. "You'd better eat more carrots."

She was thankful to see Lila and Alberta down the hall. She called loudly to them to wait and, without a glance in Norbett's direction, ran down the corridor to them.

She felt dazed and numb from Norbett's well-aimed blow, but she wouldn't let on. Not even to herself. Just as that time years ago when she'd fallen from their apple tree, she had stood up and said, "It doesn't hurt a bit—not a bit!" It hadn't hurt so bad at first—and then pain had throbbed through her bruised and wrenched knee. . . .

Mary Fred talked louder than any of the girls about what everyone was wearing to the Formal. Alberta was all indignation because her sewing teacher wanted her to put her dress in the school exhibit this week down in the Ad Building. "It was bad enough her displaying it to everyone here at Harkness," Alberta said aggrievedly. "I told her I wanted to show it off myself the night of the prom."

"Didn't it ever occur to you that he wants to get on the good side of Martie Malone so he'll have Coach Hibbs give him one of the fattest plums up at State?"

Mary Fred yelled loudly to Janet, who came hurrying out with her psychology notebook, "What about your dress for the hop, Janet?" As though she didn't already know. Janet wasn't getting a new dress. There'd been an operation in her family which cut too deeply into the budget. It was always that way at the McKean home. But Janet wore a hand-me-down from one of her well-to-do cousins and took it all in her crinkly-eyed stride. "Just wait till you see me—

red taffeta *bouffant*. Lift up the skirt and take out a telephone."

Lila had no enthusiasm over her dress. Her mother had picked it out. "It's white—so girlish and sweet. Just like you wear when you finish junior high. Puffed sleeves. It's stinko."

"In case you don't know, it's called subsidizing and it makes a lot of difference to football players who want to go on to college."

Mary Fred laughed very loudly at Lila's remark.

Alberta was saying, "With the orchid-colored bow on my skirt, an orchid on the shoulder wouldn't be bad. Thought waves, thought waves, carry that to big, dumb Pete! An orchid! An orchid!"

Janet said, "It'll be just like my Lochinvar to send pink roses to snuggle against my red taffeta."

Lila said colorlessly, "Mother'll see to it that Freddy— or should I say Freddy's mother?—sends a yellow corsage. Corny in more ways than one, eh what?"

They would have lingered at the corner where Alberta and Janet turned off, but Mary Fred said hurriedly, "So long, gals." She had to get away before they started prying information about corsages from her.

The wind seemed suddenly cold and Mary Fred shivered.

"Dike Williams is one of these poor but ambitious boys."

She almost cried out loud, "It doesn't hurt—not a bit."

Lila walked on with Mary Fred past her own house. Mary Fred knew with an added premonitory ache that Lila had something to say to her and she knew, with premonitory fear, that she didn't want to hear it.

Lila asked with the worried solicitude she so often felt for

79

Mary Fred, "Did Dike ask you to go to the Formal, Mary Fred?"

Mary Fred's very unhappiness made her fling out sharply, "Do you mean have I got it in writing? No, I haven't."

"I'll tell you why I asked," Lila went on. "Because his old girl, Sylvia, is in my chem class—she has to take chem over because she flunked it—and Dike came up to lab today and she talked to him in the doorway. And they were having sort of a quarrel. No, not a quarrel exactly, but he was trying to keep her from being sore at him. I was working on my notebook and I could hear them—and it was about the Formal. She told him he was leaving her out on a limb, and he said, 'Now look, can I help it if this has dragged out longer than I thought? All I want is to get in solid with Coach Hibbs at State—because you're going up there, and I want to go, too, don't I?'"

A little moan slipped from Mary Fred. Lila's words fitted perfectly into the other picture. Dike wanted to go to State. And Martie Malone was the best friend of the coach at State. . . . But even yet Mary Fred couldn't face it. She wouldn't let on that Norbett's words were anything but his mean jealousy.

"I thought maybe," Lila said as they walked up the steps of Mary Fred's porch, "that it might make sense to you. It didn't to me."

"It doesn't," Mary Fred said swiftly and violently. "It doesn't make a lick of sense to me. Come on in, Lila, come on in. Elizabeth's downstairs now. Oh, and you ought to see all the flowers friends of hers have sent. There's one basket in the shape of a cradle with rosebuds and lilies of the valley." She couldn't talk fast enough. "And you ought to see how the little mister can smile at us now. He can't even look at Johnny without gurgling. Beany says it's Johnny's mop of hair that he thinks is a flag waving."

You could feel Elizabeth's presence downstairs. There were flowers in vases, Elizabeth's knitting on the couch—an added coziness somehow. Elizabeth called to them from the living room. She was having tea with a tall, black-eyed soldier who was holding the baby on his lap. He hurriedly climbed to his feet as the two girls came in and gave them each a wide, bashful smile at the introduction. This was Private Clancy from the airfield. Mary Fred stared at his feet —they were such big feet.

Elizabeth motioned to an open suitcase on the chair which disclosed piles of white and pale pink garments. "You can see why Private Clancy and the little mister would have trouble wearing each other's clothes, can't you? We don't know yet how we got the wrong suitcases."

Mary Fred forced some interest into her voice. "You must have been as surprised as we were when you reached for your clothes that night." To think that once it had seemed important that Elizabeth get an answer to the ad Johnny had put in the paper!

Elizabeth was saying, "He's just been telling me that they're having a big square-dance party out at the Field to-morrow night. He says his three buddies and he are strangers here and they won't have partners. I wondered, Mary Fred, if you and Lila and Janet and Alberta couldn't go out and make up their set." Elizabeth laughed. "After all, we owe the poor fellows something. Private Clancy has been razzed all week about the size of the shirts in his suitcase. And no one had shoes that didn't pinch his feet. His buddies had to divide their socks and even their shaving outfits with him."

Mary Fred heard her own lifeless voice say, "Yes, we all love to square dance."

Lila added eagerly, "Oh, it'd be super."

Mary Fred watched with that same thudding numbness as the soldier flashed his large smile on Lila—an honest, roguish smile. He said, "I'd like you to be my own partner, if you would."

Lila gasped. It was the first time a boy had taken a step toward her without her mother's capable hand pushing him, and Lila answered readily, "Oh, I'd love to. Of course I will."

Oh, but Lila's gushing couldn't hold a candle to the way she had rushed to meet Dike Williams with her heart on her sleeve!

She had to get away. She couldn't stand all this planning gabble about the square dance. Lila's mother came hurrying over and she and Elizabeth arranged that the girls could go out with Mrs. Sears in her big car. Mary Fred muttered that she must start dinner and hurried out into the kitchen. If she worked hard and fast at something maybe she could keep on pretending that the words Norbett had flung at her didn't mean a thing. "It doesn't hurt a bit," she kept saying to herself, "not a bit!"

Beany was in the kitchen in her favorite attitude, kneeling on a chair and with the rest of her hunched over the kitchen table on which was spread the picture of her dream room. Imagine anyone thinking that having a room with yellow-plaid curtains and blue walls and mahogany-stained furniture was happiness!

Beany said, "Now next month I'll get the mahogany undercoat. And today I priced a chest of drawers—unfinished.

I'll be so glad to boot out that old child's dresser—why, I have to bend over double to pull out a drawer."

Mary Fred said, "I'm going to make a seven-minute icing for that applesauce cake I made yesterday."

"It *says* seven minutes," Beany disillusioned her. "But you just have to beat it—and beat it—till your arm aches."

Mary Fred made it, beating it harder and harder. But her mind kept working with deadly accuracy, sorting over small fragments and putting them together to form the whole ugly picture. The very first day Dike had said to her, "I hear your father's a great friend of Coach Hibbs up at State." "Oh yes, he is," she had assured him. And then that night when she had asked him to Martie Malone's birthday dinner. No wonder he had been reproachful and disappointed when she telephoned to say Martie Malone wouldn't be home! No wonder he hadn't bothered to keep the date with *her*!

Her heart kept saying, "No, it isn't so—it isn't so." But her mind went on sorting other events, holding them up to her. "Listen, snooks," she even heard Dike's pleased-with-himself laugh as they sat in the governor's box that he had lied to obtain, "it's what you get that counts, not how you get it."

It hurt so! It hurt so! It hurt to think Dike Williams didn't care for her, herself, but only for her as Martie Malone's daughter. And mixed with the hurt was the awful humiliation. "If you don't know it, then you're the only one at Harkness who doesn't," Norbett had rasped out at her. What a laugh all Harkness High must be getting at her, Mary Fred Malone, going so starry-eyed over Dike Williams' attentions!

She cringed with the shame of it. Shame was different

from grief or anxiety. You could share those with the ones you loved, just as Elizabeth shared with them her anxiety over not hearing from Don. But Mary Fred could only hug her shame close.

Lila came to the kitchen door, flushed and happy. "He's going over to our house for supper. Mother likes him."

"Who?" Mary Fred asked stupidly.

"Private Clancy," Lila said softly. "Isn't he nice, Mary Fred? And he's so big—and such a wonderful laugh. Only look, don't let on to Mother that I think he's de-gee, will you?"

"No," Mary Fred promised.

De-gee was another Harkness High term that simplified a whole sentence. Its derivatives would be hazy to trace, perhaps from *the guy*. But de-gee, in Harkness High vernacular, meant simply, "He's the most wonderful thing that ever happened." The antonym for de-gee was de-gaw, spoken with an accent of raucous disgust on the last syllable.

Lila said as she left the kitchen door, "I'll let on to Mother that I think he's a clod."

Mary Fred looked up a moment later from the icing she was spreading on her cake. There was thumping on the back porch, and then Johnny and Carlton, with a sack of potatoes between them, pushed open the door. "We went out in the country," Johnny panted, "and bought these from a farmer. They're cheaper that way. We can make a lot of things out of potatoes, can't we, Mary Fred?"

"Yeh, I guess so."

"Show enthusiasm, can't you? All the potatoes we can use and they're uncracked, unbroken, unspilled!"

Part of Mary Fred longed to go to Johnny and put her

head on his high shoulder and sob out, "Oh, Johnny, I'm all cracked and spilled and broken inside. I can never go back to Harkness High and be laughed at. You'll be ashamed you're in the same school."

9

Setting a Backfire

FINALLY the evening meal was over. Johnny waved Mary Fred out of the kitchen. He was the cleaner-upper tonight. And she was glad to get out. She went out to see if Mr. Chips had tipped over his water bucket; he had a shortsighted habit of doing that.

Ander and Johnny and Mary Fred had roughly partitioned off one side of the garage for the black horse and covered the concrete floor with a heavy coating of straw. Already it had the smell of a stable—of horse and leather and saddle soap and alfalfa hay. Mr. Chips whinnied in soft welcome when she opened the door. He nuzzled her with rough affection as she came up to him.

Standing there with her arms around his warm neck, she could no longer keep back her grief. The woeful truth crushed down on her. It was all so stabbingly clear. And Norbett was right; it was the hardest fall she had ever had. Great sobs shook her.

They had partly spent themselves when she became conscious first of the smell of that pungent dark liniment Ander used on Mr. Chips, and then of Ander's presence. He said, "I'm late getting over to rub him tonight—had to stay late at school." He came closer, touched her arm which, along with Mr. Chips' neck, sheltered her tear-swollen face. He asked gently, "What happened to hurt you so, Mary Fred?"

There was no use in pretending to Ander. She took a minute to grope for her handkerchief, to let one sob jerk itself to a hiccoughing finish. Her voice was heavy and thick. "I can never go back to school again. I can't stand everyone laughing at me. And they'll all know—the night of the Formal they'll know—in case anyone doesn't know by then—" She had to stop to even her voice a little and then she went on, "I've just been wishing I'd break my leg so I'd have an excuse—or that this sore where my boot rubbed would get infected—"

"None of that makes sense," he said casually. "Tell me in words of one syllable and in chronological order."

She told him the whole story then and at the finish she said with ragged vehemence, "So you see why I *have* to quit school, why I can't face everyone there after I've made such a fool of myself. You don't know what talk is like. It's like wildfire that just sweeps on and on."

He was thoughtfully turning the bottle of liniment upside down, then rightside up. He spoke as though he were thinking aloud, "Yes, I guess talk is something like wildfire that gets clear out of hand. It can be plenty tough. I've fought a lot of them, and there's only one sure way to stop a prairie fire. And that's to set one of your own and when the fire comes to the burned place, it has to stop because it can't go any farther. They call it setting a backfire. So look here, Mary Fred, you set your own backfire."

87

"How?"

"You tell everyone yourself that Dike Williams only went with you because you were Martie Malone's daughter. You laugh about it, yourself."

Mary Fred thought that over for a minute while Ander rubbed the liniment on Mr. Chips' strained leg. "Yes, I could do that," she said slowly. "I could let on that I didn't care—that I knew all along. I could say he was still crazy about Sylvia."

"That's it!"

"Only," she said sadly, "I've told everyone I was going to the Formal—I've even talked with the others about what dress I'd wear. If I don't go they'll know that I expected Dike to take me and he let me down."

"Did you tell everyone you were going with Dike Williams or did they just take it for granted you were?"

Mary Fred's bruised mind went sorting through all those conversations in the halls, in the lunchroom, in chem lab, on the way home. "No," she murmured, "no—I don't believe I ever said right out that I was going with Dike—because I kept waiting for him to ask me. No, not even today when Norbett asked me right out, I didn't answer him yes or no—I just said I had a date."

"Okay, that's swell! Then how about having the date for the Formal with me? There's no law against going with a fellow outside of school, is there?"

"Oh no, but—but could you stand it?" Because Ander's two loves were horses and Pre-med. Ander wanted to be through Pre-med and able to enlist in the Medical Corps by the time he was twenty.

He answered honestly, "I can take it for one night. I'll get out my tux, and I'll ask Aunt Lu if she'll lend me her

big car. As I've told you many a time, Aunt Lu is swell.
And for the prom I'll kick through with a corsage in the
grand manner."

Mary Fred laughed a wan and choked chuckle. He seemed
to sense that her handkerchief was a sodden wad and he got
out his. He wiped her eyes, said as he held it to her nose,
"Here, blow hard!" And when that was accomplished he
said, "Here's the currycomb and brush. You clean up the
nag while I dose up the bum leg." He talked casually to her
while she worked of the horses they had on their Wyoming
ranch. She realized gratefully that he was helping her over
a hard place, covering, by his very matter-of-factness, her
shame. She thought, he's nice, Ander is, but he isn't pulse-
quickening, heart-lifting like Dike Williams.

Her teeth began to shiver at the unhappy trail of thought
that came with Dike. Ander patted her on the shoulder, said,
"That'll do for tonight. You scoot on in. And stop worrying
—we'll see this thing through."

She said shakily, "Well thanks—thanks for your advice
to the lovelorn."

Mary Fred climbed the stairs to Elizabeth's room. Even
her body had a flayed, ragged feel to it. She sank down on
the foot of Elizabeth's bed. The room was dimly lighted by
a soft bed lamp. Elizabeth sat in the rocker before the fire,
nursing the baby. The rocker squeaked gently as he drowsed
off to sleep. They were like a madonna picture with the firelight flickering over them. The baby's hand was the last of
him to succumb to sleep; it kept flailing back and forth until
Elizabeth folded it into her own.

Some of the room's warmth and peace enfolded Mary
Fred.

Elizabeth laid the sleeping baby on the two armchairs fixed

with pillows and blankets and drawn up beside her bed. She began unpacking the lost suitcase, putting small stacks of clothes in the dresser.

"Look, Mary Fred," she said, "this is the first nightgown we made—and look at how big we got the neck. I couldn't figure out what to do but Don suggested putting a drawstring in it." She laughed reminiscently. "He said his grandmother used to have drawstrings in his clothes. And Mary Fred, here's what Don's buddy got the baby. He got it down at the Mexican market." She held up a brightly painted Mexican doll with a tinsel-trimmed skirt and hair that might have come out of a horse's tail. "I guess the sweet old thing never heard of sanitary toys," Elizabeth added.

Elizabeth sat there with the baby clothes on her lap, happily dreaming aloud. "These baby clothes are such a part of Don's and my evenings together. Here is the blanket I learned feather-stitching on. I couldn't seem to keep my stitches even or on the right slope. And once I got it all wrong, and it was Don that noticed it. He said it was like a rail fence that one push would send over."

"Elizabeth, were you in love very many times?"

The older girl held the baby clothes and looked back over the years which preceded them. "I thought I was—and it's practically the same."

"Were you ever in love with anyone who didn't give a doggone about you?"

"Oh, lots of times," Elizabeth said matter-of-factly. "And that's like having the mumps or chicken-pox—not fatal, but painful while it lasts."

That was small comfort to Mary Fred. This feeling she had for Dike Williams, this ache because he didn't care, felt so permanent . . .

Elizabeth was reminiscent again. "Did I ever tell you about 'winning Don'—that's the way he puts it?" Her laugh bubbled over. "I was all raptures because I had my first date with him. We were going to a football game and I had a new coat and I even gave my face a cold pack—if you can imagine having your face feeling like a board half the night! —and I was to wear a big 'mum corsage. And then that fool wisdom tooth of mine started up. Well, I went anyway and when I'd open my mouth to cheer, the cold air would hurt so. And it began swelling and swelling. I tried to carry it off even though it was like a sledge hammer pounding in my jaw. And then Don saw what was the matter and he rushed me down out of the stand and downtown to a dentist friend of his. He had to lance it—and I cried—and oh, what a mess I was with one eye bleary and swollen shut. Then Don brought me home and he taught me how to gargle. And he burned his hand fixing me some broth. But that was the afternoon we knew that when you loved each other—you loved each other."

Mary Fred added flatly, "And they lived happily ever after."

Elizabeth said earnestly, "I don't think they ought to end stories like that for children. It gives them the wrong idea. There's happiness in love—oh, happiness that shakes you and enriches you, but love and marriage isn't a happy-ever-after thing. Love and marriage has so much ache and emptiness and hurt with the happiness."

"You talk so old," Mary Fred said.

"War makes you old. Because it puts so much living in such a short time. It shows up your strong spots and your weak spots." Elizabeth reached out and lifted Mary Fred's hand to her warm cheek. "You have to love anybody awfully hard these days, Mary Fred. But love is nicer if you *like* them, too. Or does that make sense?"

"Not too much," admitted Mary Fred. She hadn't thought about *liking* Dike; there was only that excited lifting of her heart just to see him coming toward her.

Mary Fred dressed the next morning with fingers as shaky as she herself was inside. Today at Harkness High she must set the backfire that was to protect her from the tongues of talk that were as destructive as tongues of flame.

The morning was gray and cold—a day without heart. She was glad to have the storm-ridden sky and biting wind as excuse for her chattering teeth as she fell into step beside Lila. Janet and Alberta joined them. Mary Fred wished one of them would open the subject of the Spring Formal. But none of them did.

Three other girls joined them as they came within sight of Harkness. If only one of them would mention something about the event, the thought of which kept Mary Fred's teeth clicking together. But no one mentioned dresses, corsages, or prom.

Mary Fred took a long breath, plunged in, "I guess maybe everyone at school thinks I'm going to the Formal with Dike Williams. But I'm not. I'm going with Ander Erhart—the nephew of Mrs. Socially-Prominent Adams next door to us."

"*You are!*" Lila's amazement italicized her words.

"But Dike Williams wanted to take you, didn't he?" someone else asked.

Mary Fred had to work hard to make her voice light. "I doubt that. Because he's really crazy about Sylvia. She's the queen." She had to bend over, pretending to fish a bit of ice out of her shoe, before she could trust her voice. "This Ander guy from the great open spaces is nice—and he asked me to go. Dike has been giving me sort of a second-hand rush because my father's Martie Malone and well up in sport circles. Oh, Dike's all right and we have fun together but I feel sorry for someone who—who'd fall hard for him."

Lila said stanchly, "One day in Design someone insinuated that Dike was just using you. But I didn't believe it."

"He's the type," Janet said promptly. "He couldn't stand up under the spoiling he got because he's a wonderful athlete. He's on the make."

Alberta evaded Mary Fred's eyes. "I heard it, too, but I didn't know you knew."

"Oh, sure!" Mary Fred said loudly. "Any fool would have known. Why, the very first afternoon he gave it away —asking me about Father being such a bosom pal of Coach Hibbs at State. He wants to go to State because Sylvia's going there. Oh gosh, yes, any fool would have known!"

They were going up the thirty-two steps into the din of Harkness High's halls, two minutes before classes started. Well there, she had touched the match to the ground under her feet which would set a backfire and stop the oncoming, consuming one! But her knees felt wabbly under her; the books in her arms were suddenly a leaden weight.

Lila, the loyal, must have sensed Mary Fred's uneasiness of heart for she reached for her hand and squeezed it hard. And Janet, the discerning, flashed her a smile and said under her breath, "We're with you, kid!"

Evidently the flame spread in all directions. At noon Mary Fred was in the lunchroom in all the clatter of dishes and voices and scraping of chairs, saving seats for Lila and

Janet and Alberta, who had stopped at the cafeteria counter. Almost without looking up she saw, or rather sensed, the broad-shoulderedness of Dike Williams making his way through the crowd toward her. Under her yellow sweater her heart began a rat-a-tat.

Dike was balancing his usual two hamburgers and a tall glass of orange juice on his plate. His black hair always looked as though a wet comb had just been run through it— as indeed it had! The comb was sticking out of the breast pocket of his loose-hanging leather jacket. He said, "What's this, my pet? I've heard ugly rumors this morning—that you're dated up for the Spring Formal with some Gene Autry gent fresh off the plains of Wyoming. And so I hasten straight to you."

Sure, you hasten straight to me, Dike, to feel me out. You're scared it isn't so, and you're hoping like blue blazes it is. You don't dare ask me straight out for fear I'd say no, and then you'd have me on your hands. And wouldn't that be terrible? Because you've already got Sylvia.

She smiled up at him. "That's it. Just wait till you see him. He's a rodeo hero with a pile of books under his arm on account of he's going to Pre-med."

The relief in Dike Williams' handsome face was as plain to Mary Fred as the purple H on his jacket. *I hope I can put on a better act than that. You pretending to be crushed. It is to laugh.* Only she didn't dare risk laughing—not with all those hurt sobs packed inside her.

"I never thought you'd let me down with such a hard thump," he said plaintively. Lila heard that as she came up with her ham sandwich. This white-bread sandwich was Lila's one defiance of maternal dominance; her mother made her eat whole-wheat bread at home.

94

"Well—anyhow," said Dike Williams, taking a huge bite out of his hamburger sandwich and edging on through the food-bearing, china-clacking melee, "you'd better save a lot of dances for me—or else!"

"As though I wouldn't!" she said, and her shaking fingers began fumbling at the string around her lunch.

For heaven's sake, stop being all shivery inside. You're on safe ground now. The talk will go just so far, and then it'll stop. Now they can't say, "Isn't it a sin for Mary Fred Malone to fall like a ton of bricks for Dike Williams when he's only giving her a run-around?" Now they'll say, "Mary Fred is going to the Formal with some other fellow. She knew all along that Dike just wanted to get next to her father so he'd say a good word to Coach Hibbs at State. Yes, and Mary Fred just laughs about it."

Mary Fred finished unwrapping her lunch, attacked it avidly. "Hey, goon," Alberta laughed, "what are you eating your cake first for?"

It was Mary Fred's own applesauce cake with the seven-minute icing. And she had thought she was eating her cheese sandwich.

10

Swing Your Pardner!

THERE was no lift to Mary Fred's feet as she walked home this day—no treading on clouds as they had those days when Dike Williams walked beside her. Mary Fred had told Lila and Janet and Alberta not to wait for her because the Spring Formal committee might hold their final meeting if they could get the members together. Mary Fred had been quite certain that the meeting would be postponed till the following afternoon, but she wanted to walk alone under the gray leaden sky with her own matching spirits.

There was something she must tell Dike and then the bond between them would be forever severed. Then he'd drop her like the proverbial hot potato. It was ironical, too, when you thought about it. That Dike Williams had wasted so much motion, so much charm, on Martie Malone's daughter, when Martie Malone wasn't the kind to boost an athlete because he was squiring his daughter. Martie Malone wasn't that kind at all. Once when there had been some election tabulating at the *Call*, he wouldn't even give the job to Johnny because he felt that another boy might be more capable.

Today Mary Fred's feet trod only gray sidewalks and cross streets, damp and slushy. The corners of her lips felt tired from holding them in a wide, forced smile all day.

At her corner Red came trotting to meet her, to nose her hand out of the pocket of her reversible so she would pat his red silken head. He looked up at her with troubled, sympathetic eyes that entreated, "What's the matter, Mary Fred?"

They approached Mrs. Adams' imposing home and the unhurting part of Mary Fred's mind remembered how Ander was always trying to act in the role of peacemaker between his Aunt Lu and the Malones. "I'd like to see you folks neighborly instead of on the outs. I think you'd cotton right up to each other if you ever stopped scrapping long enough."

As Mary Fred passed the house, Mrs. Adams came out of the door with a coat thrown hurriedly around her shoulders. She said, "Elizabeth, there's something I've been intending to speak to your father about. Is he home now?"

"I'm Mary Fred, not Elizabeth. No, Father isn't home now. He's in Hawaii." She wondered what Mrs. Adams could have to say to their father.

Mrs. Adams enlightened her. "I thought if I spoke to him about it, it would be more effective. Although I've never approved of his laxness in discipline. But I want you to understand this—you children cannot go on treating my little Tiffin the way you do!"

Mary Fred gazed at her in honest amazement. "Stop treating your little Tiffin the way we do! Well, what about Tiffin stopping his barking and nipping at our heels?"

"I've tried to break him of that," Mrs. Adams answered. "But you must admit you do everything you can to antagonize him. But I can't understand your being brutal to him.

97

He came home today pitifully bruised and all scratched."

Mary Fred was just about to expostulate that they hadn't mistreated Tiffin, when Mrs. Adams said threateningly, "I'm warning you—I won't put up with it." And, without giving Mary Fred a chance for a last remark, she went hurrying back into the house.

Mary Fred trudged on, mystified and indignant. They had often threatened the shrill-voiced, sharp-toothed Tiffin but, so far as she knew, they had never used anything except verbal threats upon him.

But the incident slipped from her mind when she opened her front door. The house was a hubbub of talk of the square dance at the Airfield—a hubbub of clothes and sewing, for Lila and Alberta and Janet were there trying on dresses with skirts full enough, as Janet said, to hide any family of six who were fleeing from justice.

"Look, Mary Fred," Elizabeth called to her. "Look at how do-ce-do Alberta looks in my square-dance dress. And Lila's mother bought her one to wear. Doesn't she look pretty in that red plaid? But don't you think the sleeves ought to be shorter?"

"And I borrowed one from my rich cousin," Janet said, "and she told me I could cut it off if it was too long. So do you know any nice canary who would like a cover for his cage out of what I'm taking off?"

"Get out your dress, Mary Fred. You know, the green flowered one Mrs. Adams made for you the same time she made this yellow for me," Elizabeth urged.

Mary Fred thought resentfully, "You couldn't even have time to let your heart break in peace around here."

"Ander's going, too," Lila said. "He knows all the calls

and he'll get the square dance to bubbling, he says. Private Clancy says he's danced them since he was ten and he'll show me all the steps."

"It isn't the red plaid that's responsible for our Lila's rosy cheeks and starry eyes," Janet explained to Mary Fred. "It's the thought of Private Clancy."

Mary Fred said heavily, "I'd better get supper early so we can get out there by seven-thirty."

Elizabeth asked, "Mary Fred, lamb, do you feel all right? You couldn't be coming down with anything, could you?"

Mary Fred answered shortly, "No—and I haven't a coated tongue."

But you said it was painful as the mumps, Elizabeth—and it's worse. It isn't localized—it's all over me—all through me. I thought Dike liked me but he only wanted to use me.

Johnny and Beany were in the kitchen. Beany had the family camera in her hand. Johnny was holding an old yellowed newspaper and he looked up from it with that faraway light in his black eyes. "Emerson and I are getting our data. Listen to this—this is how they described the old Cherry Creek flood:

> . . . while the full-faced queen of night shed showers of silver from the starry throne o'er fields of freshness and fertility, garnishing and suffusing sleeping nature with her balmy brightness, fringing the feathery cottonwoods with lustre, enameling the house tops with coats of pearl, bridging the erst placid Platte with beams of radiance and bathing the arid sands of Cherry Creek with dewy beauty— a frightful phenomenon sounded in the distance—"

99

Mary Fred was opening the icebox. "Looks like arid sands in there," she said.

Beany was frowning at the camera. "Johnny, pipe down. Now, are you sure this is the thing you click over—not too fast and not too slow?"

"That's it, little one," Johnny said. His mind left the tragic flood of May, '64, and came back to the present and the empty icebox in the Malone kitchen. "This is Tuesday —and we have Wednesday, Thursday, and so on until Monday follows Sunday as Mondays do."

"How much have we got left in the old oatmeal box?" Mary Fred asked.

Johnny peered into the round pasteboard box. "Three dollars and some change," he said and added,

> Life is real and life is earnest,
> And the Malones still have to eat.
> We still have eggs—we have potatoes—

Beany supplied the last line, "But you can't call them a treat."

"Eggs," defended Johnny, "the food richest in vitamins. What other food can you whip up light as an April cloud and flavor with lemon—" He broke off. "By golly, that gives me an idea!" He took himself out of the kitchen and into the telephone booth under the stairs.

Beany asked, "How would you address something to Believe-it-or-not Ripley?"

"Oh, I don't know," Mary Fred said absently. "I guess you'd address it in care of the paper, or maybe they could give you his address."

"I'll call them and ask them if Johnny ever gets through on the telephone."

Johnny came out in a few more minutes, waving a paper he had covered with writing on both sides. Mary Fred said, "Johnny, I'll get supper tonight. I'll make a big pot of potato soup—that'll be good for Elizabeth. She's supposed to have a lot of milk dishes. And we can have egg-and-tomato salad."

"Swell!" Johnny said. "You get it tonight and I'll take over tomorrow night. I'll bet you don't know what I've got here. I'll bet you don't know whom I was talking to. To Pierre, the master chef, down at the Press Club. It isn't everyone he'd give his recipe to for his Lady Eleanor cake!"

"Fifteen egg whites," Beany said. "And then what'll you do with all those egg yolks?"

"That, my little chickadee, is where the artist comes in. But I won't tell you beforehand, except to say that be prepared tomorrow evening to be lifted to the heights by a meal always to be referred to as gourmet's—aye, gourmand's—delight." He looked at the two of them, asked, "Can't your souls lift a little in anticipation?"

Beany only grunted and Mary Fred said, "The coil spring to my soul is sagging somehow."

"I wondered," Johnny said, looking at her closely, "if you could be coming down with anything. Let me take your pulse. Stick out your tongue."

"Oh, hush!" Mary Fred said. "What would I be coming down with? You brought home all the diseases known to mankind."

Lila, Janet, and Alberta all ate supper at the Malones. Lila's mother sent over a platter of sliced ham and a plate of oatmeal macaroons.

"Oatmeal macaroons," orated Johnny. "Now, I contend they're far more artistic if made in the shape of a world continent. Educational as well as gustatorial." And that, as was intended, brought attention to Beany's bête noire, mounted and hung on the wall, and again Mary Fred, seeing the thirst for revenge in Beany's eyes, thought, "Johnny, my boy, you'd better watch out. If Beany gets anything on you, you'll never live it down."

They dressed for the dance in Mary Fred's and Elizabeth's suite of two rooms, with the little mister lying on Elizabeth's bed atop the rabbit blanket Johnny bought and smiling up into any eyes which looked into his.

Elizabeth said, "We want to wait till Father comes back to christen him."

"But even so, you should decide on a name and call him that," scolded diminutive Janet, the psychology student. "Even tiny babies shouldn't be called 'the baby' or 'the little fellow.' They should be made to feel they're individuals."

"But we can't decide between Donald Martin and Martin Donald. We don't know whether to call him Martie or Don," apologized Elizabeth.

Lila's mother was already waiting downstairs, and Ander had come over wearing a wide, white sombrero, a bright yellow shirt, and cowboy chaps, before the four girls had the last button buttoned on their snug basques and their long ruffly skirts adjusted.

Elizabeth detained them for one last word of admonition. "Now listen, gals, be sure you go out there to this soldiers' dance with only one idea—not to have a good time yourselves but to give them one. Because you've got other good times ahead of you. But these kids—we don't know what's ahead for them. They're away from home and they're homesick and girlsick—oh, you'll have to listen to them tell about their girls!—and some of them are awful dancers. But just forget about yourselves. Though I suppose it's hard for youth not to be selfish," she added.

Mary Fred grinned at them all as she kissed Elizabeth's soft cheek. "She's old and doddering," Mary Fred said. "She's nineteen. 'Bye, Little Mom. We'll spread cheer."

Some four hours later when Mary Fred tiptoed in, Elizabeth wakened and asked softly, "How was it?"

Mary Fred always undressed in Elizabeth's warm room with its nice smell of baby talcum, castile soap, and wool blankets. Tonight the dying firelight vaguely caught on the sparkling buttons which Mary Fred's listless fingers pushed backwards through their buttonholes, on the tired brightness of her eyes. "It was Lila's night," Mary Fred said. "She and Clancy each think the other is the answer to all their morning and evening prayers. He's rich on blarney—that Clancy—and Lila swallows it—hook, line, and sinker." A small shiver passed through the partly undressed figure. "A girl shouldn't do that."

"I think he means it," Elizabeth said. "When he first saw her he seemed to get a great glow. Were the dances fun?"

"Ander was a wow at calling them. He called one that seemed inspired by Clancy:

> Lady, swing that gent that looks so neat,
> Now the one whose breath is sweet,
> Now the one with the great big feet—

and Lila said right out, 'Why, they're not so big!' It was a roar."

"Ander's nice," Elizabeth mused. "He has a test coming up tomorrow and yet he took time out to go out there and liven it up for the soldiers. Did he dance any—with you?"

"Just a few," Mary Fred said absently, "to show us all some of his fanciest figures." Mary Fred yawned heavily. "Janet had a great time psychoanalyzing her partner. She said he had a mother-complex because all he could talk about was the way his mother made Swedish meat balls."

"He was probably hungry. Did you have a regular pardner?"

"You mean did I make a heart beat faster under his shirt of khaki? No. I mothered all the ones that looked lonesome. I oh'd and ah'd over hundreds of snapshots of 'the girl I left behind me.' I let the poor dancers walk on my feet. I had no thought of self."

Elizabeth laughed softly. The baby stirred. "Get to bed, you lug."

Mary Fred scampered out to her own chilly sleeping quarters. She opened her windows to let in some of the cold night wind blowing from a black sky with pale stars. In the house next door she could see Ander's slim outline as he sat at his desk studying for the test tomorrow. Three hours of boning, he said, for a test in Dynamic Chem.

11

Lady Eleanor Cake

MARY FRED had to stay after school the next afternoon for the final committee meeting of the Spring Formal. There was much discussion as to whether they should get ices molded in the shape of lilies or conserve their funds and serve brick ices in spring colors, pale yellow and green.

Mary Fred spoke up—it was as though Elizabeth were beside her, prompting her—"I suggest that we spend less on our ices and, if we have any money left, donate it to the entertainment fund for the soldiers."

And the committee accepted her suggestion.

Again this late afternoon as Mary Fred walked heavy-heartedly past the home of Mrs. Socially-Prominent Adams, that woman came hurrying out of her house, and again her tone was challenging. "Little Tiffin has disappeared."

Mary Fred longed to say, "Why, how nice!" but instead she said, "That's too bad."

But evidently Mrs. Adams caught the note of sarcasm in

even that innocent remark for she said angrily, "Of course, I have my own idea as to whom to suspect. What have you done with him?"

Mary Fred answered shortly, "We haven't done anything with him. But I know what I'd like to do." And she walked on.

She remembered, as she turned in at their gate, that Elizabeth had planned to take the baby and go riding with a friend of hers, so Mary Fred walked around to the back door. The Malones always felt perfectly safe if they locked the front door when they went out, because they could depend on Red to lie on the back step. He lay there this afternoon, covering the whole step, his ears and eyes watchful. He lifted his head, making room for Mary Fred's feet, and greeted her with a happy, tail-thumping dignity which said, "You may pass."

On the kitchen door was a scribbled note from Johnny:

Carl and I heard of a fellow on Broadway that can maybe fix the spacer on typewriter. Lady Eleanor cake in oven.

The last sentence was quite unnecessary. For, as Mary Fred opened the door, a burned smell greeted her, and small wisps of smoke curled out of the crack around the oven door. When Mary Fred yanked open the oven, a black cloud spumed forth. She grabbed for a potholder, pulled out a blackened cake pan and its charred contents. So that was the Lady Eleanor cake!

With one hand she deposited it on top of the stove and with the other reached across the sink's drainboard to throw up the window. She pulled shut the door leading into the dining room, hoping to keep the smoke out of the rest of the house.

At that moment Johnny came rushing in the back door. "When I turned the corner," he panted, "I could see the smoke pouring out of the window—and I remembered Lady Eleanor!"

Mary Fred giggled weakly. "What a Lady Eleanor we have with us this afternoon!" They looked at it in consternation. The cake had raised and rounded before it had burned to blackness. It was a gently rounded, ebony-black mummy of a cake.

Johnny was murmuring, "Pierre said it would take quite a while to bake. He said to allow plenty of time for it to bake through."

"You did," Mary Fred remarked.

Johnny mourned on as they stared at the burnt cake. "I made the green noodles; that was the chef's other secret. He gave me that recipe so as to use up the yolks. Noodles à la Naples! See there, Mary Fred." He motioned to the table where finely cut, olive-green noodles lay drying. "I cooked a whole kettle of spinach and cooked down the water till it was concentrated—"

"Did you save the spinach for tomorrow?" Mary Fred asked with some of Beany's practicality.

"Yes, I did. Pierre said the noodles would green up more in cooking. And I'm going to make a cheese sauce for the noodles that Pierre said was something to dream about. But the cake was to have been the crowning glory of the meal."

Their grieving inaction came to a sudden end. "Jiggers!" Johnny said. "Here comes Beany! Gosh, she'd never stop gloating if she saw the cake. Where can we hide the *corpus delicti?*"

Mary Fred grabbed up the black pan containing the cinder cake. She couldn't run outdoors because Beany was coming in the back way and would catch her red-handed—or black-handed. So she dashed down in the basement with it. Under the basement stairs was a closet which was the catchall for unused rolls of wallpaper and half-empty cans of varnish. Into this closet Mary Fred thrust the pan and its contents and swiftly shut the door.

She didn't quite make it back to the kitchen. She was on the second step from the top when Beany opened the door. The younger sister stood in the doorway like an accusing, triumphant god. "What burned?"

"What burned?" repeated Johnny. "Why—nothing."

"Nothing burned!" challenged Beany, sniffing with her small, upturned nose like a hound dog on a scent. "I could see the smoke as I came in the yard. I thought the house was on fire. What have you got the window wide open for if nothing burned?"

Mary Fred was not only too out of breath to answer, but she wasn't as quick a thinker as Johnny. "The window?" Johnny repeated innocently. "Oh, we just opened it to air out. There were a few crumbs in the oven—you know how toast makes crumbs—and they kind of burned when I lit the oven."

Of course Beany didn't believe it! She opened the oven door, and her eyes probed into it. She looked avidly about the kitchen for evidence.

"Well," said Johnny, very businesslike, "guess I'd better get my Noodles à la Naples on. You know the rule, Beany, my pet, them as ain't cooking has to get out of the kitchen. Besides, I asked Emerson Worth out to share our meal delectable. You look after him when he comes."

"Oh, him and his giants walked the streets in those days!" said Beany disgruntledly.

"Tell him," prompted Johnny, "that Miss Hewlitt thinks the book we're launching will be one our grandchildren will be proud of."

He had to shoo Beany out. Then he and Mary Fred looked at each other. They knew that Beany was only temporarily removed. Beany was still on the scent.

Under cover of running water, Johnny said, "We got to get that chunk of carbon clear out of the house."

"I'll say we have."

"She'd probably mount it under a glass dome in the living room," Johnny mused. "She'd never let us live it down."

Mary Fred thought that *us* a little strong—but after all they had promised to pardner it for better or for worse. "We'll have to wait till it's dark," she said.

All the time they boiled the green noodles, grated the cheese for the velvety sauce, they felt Beany's removed but watchful presence.

Elizabeth returned from her drive. She was no sooner in the front door than she sniffed inquiringly. "Is something burning?"

"Something *did* burn," Beany said. Her tone added a postscript, "And I'm going to find out what."

Old Emerson Worth said the same thing as Beany took his hat and he reached up to loosen his white muffler. "Is something burning?"

"Not right now," said Beany.

Emerson Worth looked as though he had missed Martie Malone's looking after him. In his frayed overcoat and battered hat, he was like a shabby old rooster who has only his strut left. And Emerson's strut was his white silk muffler, his grandiloquent manner, his wing collar. This evening he was deeply troubled over the world news. The headlines on the *Call* were not encouraging. "It's the people of today," he said. "They want to get things the easy way."

Behind his back Beany soundlessly shaped these words: "Oh, for the giants of those early days!"

Emerson Worth looked long at the baby Elizabeth brought to show him, before he said with slow impressiveness, "If that isn't little Martie Malone, I'll eat my hat."

A smile passed like a handclasp around the group as the same thought crossed all their minds; then it had better be little Martie Malone, for Emerson's green-with-age hat looked far from digestible. "Thank you, Emerson, for deciding," Elizabeth said graciously. "We couldn't make up our minds. Martie it is."

Once while Johnny and Mary Fred were working in the kitchen they saw Beany slip furtively past the kitchen window. Johnny looked out through the glass in the back door and reported, "She's poking around her rabbit's box—and another wooden box out there by the ashpit."

"That's funny," Mary Fred said. "I thought sure she guessed it was in the basement."

Still another guest came. Ander knocked on the back door and asked, "Have you folks seen anything of Aunt Lu's little pocket-sized pooch?"

Mary Fred, who was concocting a fruit dessert to fill the gap left by the Lady Eleanor cake, answered shortly, "No, we haven't. But, if you'd like, you can search the place. What does she think we'd do with little Tiffin?"

He said reprovingly, "Don't get on the prod, young lady."

Mary Fred laughed, but her voice was edgy. "It is to laugh! You playing the part of the Dove of Peace, telling us that your aunt is a lonely, heart-of-gold person and that we're to blame for not being neighborly, and every time I walk past her house, she rushes out and accuses me of being a sadist and maltreating her dog."

Johnny was hunkered down before the open oven, and he lovingly edged out the bubbling and browning casserole to show Ander. "Noodles à la Naples. It'd be an epoch in your life to eat them. Suppose you and Mary Fred stop scrapping long enough for you to join us."

Ander said, "I'll take you up on that. Aunt Lu has been so upset that no one at our house can settle down to a meal. I drove her downtown to put an ad in the paper under 'Lost and Found.' I don't know of anything else I can do," he ended gravely.

Mary Fred had the parting thrust, "You could go into mourning."

Praise was extravagant for the green noodles and the velvety cheese sauce. Only Beany sat there with a resolute gleam in her eye. She suspected, of course, that the evidence was somewhere in the basement, and all she needed was time to find it.

During the commotion at the meal's breaking up, Johnny begged Elizabeth, "For heaven's sake, send Beany upstairs to do something for the baby. Five minutes is all we ask."

Mary Fred listened to Beany's steps hurrying up the stairs to see if the baby was too well covered or not covered enough, and then Mary Fred's feet sped down the basement steps. She groped in the closet amongst the clutter till her hand touched the edge of the pan. It was still uncomfortably warm, but she grabbed it up, using the edge of her skirt as potholder. Johnny opened the side door for her and she dashed out.

The ashpit would receive their secret; the ashes and trash in the ashpit would cover it. Then she and Johnny could breathe easily.

She was running through the darkness when she stumbled over a wooden box. She stumbled against it with such force that she not only went sprawling on her knees but knocked the box over on its side and sent it skidding some three feet over the frozen ground.

And instantly there arose that shrill familiar frenzy of barking; there came that familiar onrush at her heels.

Mary Fred was just getting to her feet when their back door was swung wide. The commotion was enough to rouse the whole neighborhood. In her surprise at the little brown dog making darting passes at her, she completely forgot she was still clutching the black pan with its black contents.

The whole Malone family was pouring out the back door. From the front walk came other hurrying feet, and Mary Fred blinked as she found herself in the bright, revealing glare of a flashlight turned full upon her. A woman's voice, catchy and hysterical, was calling, "Tiffin—Tiffin, where are you?"

There was such a bedlam then of Tiffin's yelps and Mrs. Adams' repeating, "He's hurt—the poor little thing! Oh, he's hurt!" that Ander took the little dog out of his aunt's arms and said, "Come on in where it's light and we'll see."

It seemed a little strange for Mrs. Socially-Prominent Adams to be standing under the light in the Malone front hall with all the Malones gathered about her. (Only the Malone guest, Emerson Worth, was dozing on the front-room couch.)

Ander turned the quivering, whimpering little dog this

way and that. He patted him gently, scoldingly. "Pipe down, fellow, pipe down." And Tiffin did subside to an aggrieved whine. "I think Mary Fred fell on him," Ander explained, "and that, along with her kicking the box about, scared the poor dog to death."

"What was Tiffin doing under the box?" Mary Fred asked bewilderedly.

Mrs. Adams accused them all, "You had him here all the time I was hunting for him and worrying over him—you had him here. And denied it point-blank."

Ander asked bluntly, "Who the dickens did put him under a wooden box?"

A little squawk sounded from Beany. "I did," she admitted. "Only he didn't mind—honest, he didn't. He liked it. And I thought that when you saw his picture in the paper —in all the national papers even, you'd be so proud. Wait till I show you!" She ran out to the shelf in the kitchen and returned with a snapshot. "See here! I took this yesterday but you can't see it very plain—because it was cloudy, I guess. You know it's been cloudy after school for I don't know how long. It wasn't so very cloudy this evening, but when I came home and smelled something so awfully burned, I forgot about taking it until it was too late. I went out once and by then it was too darkish." Beany's usually rosy face was pale and she was breathing hard as she looked appealingly at them all. But she was careful not to look at the accusing figure of Mrs. Adams.

The gray blurry snapshot was passed from one to the other. It wasn't until Mary Fred went to reach for it that she realized she was still clutching the burnt cake in its burnt pan. She edged farther into the corner behind Johnny.

Elizabeth took the picture and held it under the light and stared at it closely. "Why, it's your Frank rabbit, isn't it, Beany?"

"Yes," Beany agreed, happy that someone had recognized it. "That white spot is Frank. And see that other sort of spot by him. That's Tiffin. Only I'll have to get a better one to send in to Believe-it-or-not Ripley, but I thought if the sun came out in the morning—and I don't think I pulled that little jigger on the camera fast enough."

"What are you talking about?" Mrs. Adams asked.

"It's a picture I want to send in to Believe-it-or-not Ripley," Beany explained as though everyone were stupid but her. "But nobody could take a picture when the sun doesn't stay out long enough."

"And you let Aunt Lu worry herself to death so you could take a picture of those two together?" Ander asked. "Why, Beany, didn't you hear me tell that she couldn't eat any supper, and that we drove down to put an ad in the 'Lost and Found'?"

Both Johnny and Mary Fred defended her swiftly. "No, Beany wasn't in the kitchen when you told that."

Beany said guiltily, "I didn't think she'd worry very much. I thought I'd tell her all about it when I had the picture."

Beany stammered out her story in roundabout fashion. How Tiffin had somehow been drawn to the white rabbit in antagonistic fascination. "They had some awful fights," Beany said, "until Frank put Tiffin in his place. And then they were friends. Of course, I always liked Frank after a fashion but I never respected him before. But this kind of restored my faith in all rabbits—to think he wouldn't let Tiffin dominate him. You see," she said earnestly, "for generations people have said 'scared as a rabbit' and 'meek as a rabbit' and I wanted to prove that all rabbits aren't scared and meek. I wanted to send a picture of a dog and a rabbit playing together to Ripley. Our Red tolerates Frank but he never treats him as an equal."

There was silence in the hall. It was a tense, waiting silence. The years of petty antagonism and enmity between the Malones and their next-door neighbor, whom they delighted in calling Mrs. Socially-Prominent Adams because she called them the awful Malones, seemed to hang suspended. The situation could go one way or the other. A word could break the enmity; a word could heighten it. Mary Fred felt that Ander, more than anyone else, was anxious that it should swing to friendliness.

Each of the Malones looked at the other. They were too proud to eat humble pie for Mrs. Adams. And yet Beany shouldn't have kept the dog! Mary Fred looked at Elizabeth and breathed an inward sigh of relief. For Elizabeth, the generous, the soft-spoken, was taking a step toward Mrs. Adams. She even said, "I'm sure Beany didn't mean—"

But a thumping commotion on the porch distracted everyone's attention. Johnny, being closest, opened the door. Company was arriving, bag and baggage—and what a lot of swanky baggage!—at the Malones'.

12

Fairy Godmother

FOR a brief moment or two all the Malones, congregated there in the hall, gaped as a taxi driver made two extra trips to the taxi, bringing back luggage which he piled into the hall under the supervision of a woman plainly dressed in a dark blue suit and sensible oxfords. Why, that was Hattie, who was at the same time maid, housekeeper, and secretary for their step-grandmother, Nonna! On those fleeting visits Nonna had paid them Hattie had accompanied her.

And the other woman, who was not at all plainly dressed, was Nonna. Her lapis lazuli earrings called attention to her eyes which were that same deep blue. Her black hat framed her silvery blond hair. Mary Fred got an impression of silveriness. A silvery gray fur half fell off her shoulders. As she pulled off her gloves you heard the clink of silver bracelets. Even her laugh, as she took a step toward Mary Fred, had a silvery tinkle. "My dears, how startled you all look! Are you so surprised to see your Nonna? I warned you, you know, that I was coming one of these days."

Greetings flew fast, with Nonna's explaining in small

chunks between greetings that she had sold her decorating business in Philadelphia very suddenly. "And I thought I'd come back to my home town. You poor lambs, you'll never know how guilty I felt, leaving you out here without a mother."

Elizabeth introduced Nonna to Mrs. Adams and to Ander. Nonna looked at Mrs. Adams and smiled not entirely pleasantly. "I believe I already know Mrs. Adams. Weren't you Lu Watkins who lived in the little reddish-brown house next to the grocery store there on Twelfth?"

Any chance of conciliation between the Malones and Mrs. Adams was shattered by that gently edged remark. Mrs. Adams said coldly, "Yes, I was Lu Watkins. But I didn't live in a reddish-brown house—it was yellow—and it was three houses from the grocery." She turned to Ander and said, "We'd better get Tiffin home where we can take care of him. He's suffered enough."

Ander turned at the door to give Mary Fred what seemed a look of reproach.

But all Mary Fred's thoughts were concentrated on making an unobtrusive getaway with the burnt cake before the hubbub died down and someone noticed what she was clutching. She measured the distance between herself and the door into the front room and edged toward it, holding the cake behind her.

The plan might have worked perfectly but for another individual in the front room who desired to edge unobtrusively into the group in the hall. Emerson Worth. There was this about Emerson Worth's naps. He would never admit that he went to sleep sitting up there on the end of the couch. He always rejoined the group and the conversation as though he had never been out of it.

And so, just as Mary Fred backed out through the living room door, she bumped into the old man, and the cake pan, held gingerly behind her, dropped, and the black cake was at last dislodged from the pan.

Old Emerson Worth stooped and picked up the cake and stood looking at it in puzzled fashion. "It looks like a cinder brick—except that it's not uniform in shape. Could this be a relic of the old Denver fire?"

All the group, except Johnny and Mary Fred, were looking at it with the same puzzled wonder.

"What in the world is it?" Nonna asked.

Johnny said unhappily, "It's a Lady Eleanor cake."

"A Lady Eleanor cake!" she exclaimed with her tinkly laugh. "Not that?"

Beany said impatiently, "For heaven's sake, Johnny, go on out and dump it in the ashpit. No use everybody gawping at it."

Johnny said meekly, gratefully, "Okay, Beany. And while I'm about it, I'll throw out that relief map in the dining room. Don't know as we want everybody gawping at that either."

And that was that!

Finally all the pieces of baggage were out of the hall. Nonna would occupy the guest room upstairs and Hattie would use the room in the basement that Mrs. No-Complaint Adams stayed in. Mary Fred hurried to telephone her that she would not need to stay the night with them, now that they had a step-grandmother and her Hattie with them.

Beany asked Mary Fred in a whisper, "How long is she going to stay—Nonna?"

"Why, Beany, the idea of wondering that when someone has just come! You sound as though you didn't like her."

Beany evaded unhappily, "I don't like anybody who looks like one thing and is something else."

Mary Fred knew what she meant. Nonna had a frail, almost flowerlike beauty; her voice was gentle and her eyes were limpid and soft. Yet under it was drive, efficiency. It hadn't taken her long to get herself and Hattie and their belongings settled.

Beany went on, "I don't like the way she looked at old Emerson Worth—like he was something she wanted to sweep out."

Evidently old Emerson hadn't liked it either. Usually when he came out to dinner he stayed the night. The Malones always urged him to, for his rooming house was a dreary and drab two stories of unclean halls, and his room a small square containing an iron bed, an uncomfortable chair, and boxes overflowing with books he had never completely unpacked.

This evening he and Johnny had planned an evening's work on The Book. "We'll do the chapter on the Cherry Creek flood," Johnny had said, his long nervous fingers tapping together. "When Emerson Worth was a boy he used to know one of the prisoners who was in the city jail that night it was washed down. I can hardly wait to put down what he tells about it."

But Nonna had no more than taken gentle, but firm, command when Emerson had hurried into his overcoat, clutched uneasily at his hat, and, without taking careful, shaky-fingered deliberation in adjusting his white silk muffler, was off with only a muttered goodbye.

Beany said, "You don't suppose she's going to *stay* here, do you?"

"How should I know?" Mary Fred said.

But as Nonna parted from Hattie for the night, Mary Fred overheard, "Well, Hattie, it looks as though our work is laid out for us here."

"Yes, it does, Mrs. Gaylord."

Lila was waiting on their accustomed corner the next morning. She greeted Mary Fred with a complimentary gasp. "Mary Fred, you've got a new jacket! It's scrumptious!"

"It's a present from Nonna. It came from New York." The jacket was of bright Kelly green, soft and fuzzy and warm, and Mary Fred's voice reflected the brightening of her spirits. "I feel like spring—hope pushing through the dark clod—the sap running, and all that."

Janet fell into step with them in time to hear that. "It's the psychological lift clothes give you, especially bright red or bright green," she said, and added with her crinkly smile, "You're pretty, you little nut."

But not pretty enough or queen enough for Dike Williams, Mary Fred thought with that old jab of pain.

She bubbled on recklessly, "And that's not all. I'm a pampered young thing. I'm the idle rich. I'm a queen. Can you imagine it! I only got up in time to eat my breakfast and take off to school. Barely had time to shake out some oats for Mr. Chips. Mary Fred Malone steps out of the laboring class."

"Didn't your alarm go off?" Lila asked.

"It didn't go off because Nonna turned it off after I was asleep. She said I needed that extra sleep. Nonna's wonderful. I felt like a heel going off to school and leaving such an upset house. But how I soaked up that extra hour of sleep!

I feel more fit to cope with life's problems this morning."

Her voice wavered, with all its jubilance gone. Life had a problem ahead and she didn't feel entirely fit to cope with it. The Spring Formal on Saturday night. She had to carry it off. She had to pretend that she didn't care in the least because Dike was there with Sylvia. She pulled the bright green jacket close about her, wanting every bit of psychological lift it could give.

The next morning Mary Fred continued her enthusiastic praise. "I tell you Nonna's too good to be true. It's like magic the way she's taken over. You remember my telling about our taking off to school and leaving the house so helter-skelter? But when we came home from school yesterday, all was serenity and shining order. And the most heavenly food smells. And Beany's blouses, that we never can keep more than one ahead, all ironed and folded on her bed with every button on. Just like a high-class laundry. My closet was all cleaned. Nonna said she wanted to see what filling-in my wardrobe needed."

Alberta was nervously studying the notes of a fashion show she was to report on in Design this morning. But the word "wardrobe" roused her. "Those spring corduroys. Tell her they'd fill any gap in a wardrobe. Tangerine, lime, raspberry—umm, they're luscious enough to eat!"

But Lila went back to the magic Nonna had wrought in the house. "Did she do all that cleaning and cooking and ironing Beany's blouses?"

"She had a cleaning woman come in, and she had Hattie. Nonna is the executive type."

Janet said with strange contrariness, "When I come over I'm going to call her grandma just to prick that vanity complex of hers."

"But she isn't a grandmother type of person," Mary Fred defended. "She's more like a fairy godmother. Out from one of the downtown stores comes a special delivery—she's the kind who always has things marked 'Special'—and it's the loveliest bassinet for Elizabeth's baby. Nonna thought it would be nicer than to have him sleeping on the two chairs Elizabeth fixed by the side of her bed with a pillow on them. Nonna says she wants to do for us."

Alberta continued, "If she does get you a spring corduroy —this fairy step-grandmother—my jealous hands will claw it off of you."

"But what about your housework arrangements?" Janet asked. "Aren't you going to do the housework so as to have the money?"

"Nonna says we don't need to. We told her about the arrangements and she said it was all foolish and unnecessary. She said it was too much work and responsibility for us. We told her Father had put us on our own and that Johnny had a repair bill to pay, and that he craved a typewriter for his literary pursuits. And I told her about buying Mr. Chips—"

"I'll bet she got a thrill out of Mr. Chips," Janet put in dryly.

"She said we weren't to worry over a thing—that she'd provide for us."

Lila said troubledly, "You Malones have always done the deciding and providing for yourselves. I've always envied you."

Mary Fred said, "But it was an awful chore. Having to get up early to do the work before school and then go hurrying home—"

"With Dike Williams taking up so much time," Janet amended.

A slang phrase went through Mary Fred: "Them days is gone forever."

She continued defending herself, "And we had all that worry of wondering if the money would stretch out. And those awful eggs! And trying to figure out different ways to cook potatoes. It's heaven to have Nonna take over."

Janet said, "How about that quotation you cut your teeth on—'The highest price you can pay for a thing is to get it for nothing'?"

"Nonna put it this way," Mary Fred explained. "She said that if she took Hattie and stayed at a hotel it would cost her much more than if they stayed with us and she paid the running expenses, and that she was happier being with us and doing for us. She says she's been working hard and making money and now she wants to run a home and have some of the social life she left when she moved away from here. She was a Gaylord and I guess the Gaylords were—sort of—"

"Socially prominent, my pet," Janet said. "She and your Mrs. Morrison Adams can be nip-and-tuck."

Mary Fred chuckled. "Evidently there was some nip-and-tuck between them in years gone by, because Nonna was ready the minute she met her with a nip about her living in a little house near a grocery store, which, it seemed to me, would be very handy. Anyway, Nonna and Hattie are planning some teas and receptions for Nonna's old friends."

"Who's this Hattie, this woman Friday of hers?" Alberta asked, her attention coming to the surface again after another dip into her fashion report.

"That's about it. Hattie's so capable and quiet. She's almost an echo of what Nonna says and thinks. She's been with her seventeen years. Imagine!"

"Sounds like a submerged personality," Janet said to that.

"Oh hush, Janet," Mary Fred said. "Elizabeth said that Hattie told her she took a beauty course and she thought she'd go back to her little home town and set up a shop. But when she finished the course she couldn't get a job. And she started working for Nonna just temporarily. And she's still with her."

They were at the steps of Harkness High. Most of the student body stood about in the sun, waiting for the last bell to draw them in. The words "Spring Formal" were peppered about in the conversation of the different groups. Again Mary Fred felt the cold push of uneasiness under her ribs. This was Friday morning. Every day this week had been a hard and frightening hurdle to be got over. But the night of the Formal—oh, that was the highest, scariest hurdle of them all!

In the Malone home Nonna's fairy wand continued to wave. When Mary Fred reached home that evening she found Hattie taking care of the baby. Nonna had taken Elizabeth to a tea.

As Mary Fred trudged up the stairs with her books, Johnny came out of his room. "Mary Fred," he said, awed. "I've got it."

"What?"

"Come and see."

On Johnny's desk, the mission table which had been painted blue and then given such hard usage that the blue paint chipped off, showing the blackish finish beneath, sat a shining new typewriter. Johnny dallied his fingers over the keys. His long brown hands looked grubby and ink smudged and out of place against such gleaming newness. "This is the tabulator. Listen to how quiet the keys do their stuff. Makes me feel like I ought to whisper—or else wash behind my ears. And the spacer—one space and no more. No hop, skip, or jump with this spacer." Yet Johnny seemed almost more dazed than pleased.

"Thrill, thrill," Mary Fred said. "At long last your dream has come true!"

"But it doesn't seem real. To think of me getting a brand-new typewriter without turning a hand. It doesn't seem mine. Nonna went down and talked to the typewriter company and they took my old high-busted Tillie on a trade. But I'll bet they can't find out why that spacer cavorts the way it does."

"Now you can fly along on your book," Mary Fred said.

"Yes," he repeated. "Yes—now I can fly along on my book."

Nonna and Elizabeth returned a little later. They had that dressed-up and flushed prettiness that goes with partying. Elizabeth took off her coat and revealed herself in a new flowered jersey, as brightly colored as a basket of Easter eggs. Elizabeth said, "Nonna bought it for me." She turned admiringly before the glass over her dressing table. "I'm ashamed of being such a vain piece. I didn't know how hungry I was for a new dress."

Hattie was down in the kitchen seeing to dinner. Beany came in from school and, as usual, gravitated toward the bassinet where the small Martie was fanning his hands and hoping for attention.

Beany picked him up, as deftly as any mother of six, and smoothed his clothes. She said, "Why, he's got on a *dress.* All embroidered and everything! Where'd he get that?"

Elizabeth said, "Nonna sent out a whole new layette for him."

Beany said flatly, "He didn't need a new layette. With the six nightgowns Johnny got him, and the six you and Don made him, Elizabeth, he had lots and lots of clothes."

Nonna stopped in the doorway and smiled at them as she fluffed into soft becomingness her hair which her hat had flattened. "I thought it was more appropriate for him to have—well, something a little nicer. So, Elizabeth, you might make all the other baby clothes into a bundle and we'll give them to the Salvation Army."

Beany contributed stubbornly, "The nurse at St. Joseph's said it was healthier to keep nightgowns on them for the first few months. She said they were more comfortable. She said it meant more for them to be warm and quiet than to be dressed up. It was better for their whole nervous system, she said."

Beany was the only one of the Malones who had not succumbed to the great generosity, the winning charm of Nonna.

That evening Nonna said to Mary Fred, "I haven't been able to do anything for Beany. What do you think the child would like?"

"She wants to do her room over so bad she can taste it," Mary Fred said. "She just hates her room because it's so six-year-oldish."

Nonna agreed. "Yes, it's a disgrace for a decorator to live in the same house with that room. I'd be ashamed for any of my friends to see it." Her eyes narrowed in concentration. "It might be nice—on the north—in chartreuse with a touch or two of those warm fuchsia shades. I did one that was simply delectable."

"No—oh, no, Nonna," Mary Fred said in alarm. "Beany knows exactly what she wants and how she wants it. And she wants to do it herself. She's already got the yellow-plaid gingham for the curtains and a can of mahogany undercoat. She planned to buy the rest when she got her next house-keeping money."

Mary Fred regretted, for Beany's sake, that they were not continuing with the housework. Father had told them to see his friend at the bank when the month was up and draw out money for the next month's groceries and housekeeping allotment. But now they were not entitled to it.

Mary Fred repeated, "Beany knows just what she wants. The picture of her room is so worn that it won't hold together—but, even so, it's indelibly engraved on her heart."

"My dear," Nonna reproved gently, "Beany is thirteen. And I have been doing rooms for the young Biddles and Mellons and Stuyvesants for more years than I can say."

It was strange about Nonna. She never raised her voice, yet somehow one didn't argue with her.

Elizabeth had turned up the hem of the blue dress she had worn in the campus Maypole dance and, on this the night before the Spring Formal, she had Mary Fred try it on to be sure the length was right.

Mary Fred asked Nonna's opinion. Yes, Nonna agreed, the length was perfect now. "But won't a great many people recognize that dress as Elizabeth's Maypole dance dress?"

"Yes," Mary Fred conceded, "they will."

"With whom are you going to this dance, Mary Fred?"

Mary Fred's answer pushed through the disappointed pain in her chest. "With Ander Erhart, Mrs. Adams' nephew."

Nonna's laugh gave the effect of a shrug of distaste. "It amuses me to see the airs Lu Watkins—Lu Adams, she is now—puts on. And the condescending attitude she has toward you children."

"She calls us 'the awful Malones,'" Mary Fred admitted.

"Indeed? I'm surprised that she'd further any relationship between her nephew and one of the 'awful Malones.'"

"She doesn't," Mary Fred said honestly, unhappily. "Ander's just being nice to me." She laughed nervously. "The joker of it is that he's going to take me in her car, only he has to drop her off at a concert first. Just one happy family starting off."

"Do you suppose Lu Watkins saw the Maypole ceremony last spring?"

"Mrs. Adams? Oh, I'm sure she did. She goes to all the university affairs."

"Hm-mm," Nonna mused. "And she's just the kind to notice if you were wearing your sister's dress." Once again her eyes grew thoughtful with plans.

13

From Mop-Squeezer to Queen

THE next day, Saturday, was the day of the Spring Formal. Mary Fred went about with cold hands, and that cold uneasiness—fright, even—yeasting inside her.

Nonna had set out early to go downtown shopping. Elizabeth pressed the blue dress. "I just barely dampened the appliquéd roses, and see how pretty they stand out." She held the dress high on its velvet hanger and swished it about for Mary Fred's approval.

"Oh, lovely!" Mary Fred praised it. "Thanks." But an unhappy dirge in her said, "Everyone will know it's Elizabeth's hand-me-down. I don't care about that except I feel hand-me-down myself, dragging poor Ander there. And how can I carry it off that it's swell with me for Dike Williams to be there with Sylvia?"

Beany had finally finished one of the pair of yellow-plaid curtains that were to go up at her window. "Isn't the ruffle just beautiful?" Beany exclaimed. "See how the ruffle goes

129

around the corner of the curtain without pulling a bit. You have to hold a ruffle real full to turn a corner with it."

"You're so capable, Beany," Mary Fred admired, and then out of her own unhappiness, cried out, "I'm so sick of always hearing 'Elizabeth's such a lovely person, and Johnny's such a genius—and Beany's such a capable child.' And I'm not such an *anything*."

Beany said earnestly, "But you are, Mary Fred. You're such a helper, such a holder-of-us-together. We all lean on you and depend on you. I never would have thought I could do this room over if you hadn't told me I could. And Johnny —he and Emerson never would have tackled that intimate history of the State if you hadn't spurred them on."

Mary Fred wanted to snap out, "I don't want to be a helper, and a holder-together. I don't want to be leaned on."

Beany said, "Mary Fred, would you mind standing on the dresser and holding the curtain up to the window? Just so I can kind of see how it'll look—and if it will lift the sun out of the sky and bring it in?"

Mary Fred climbed onto the low wabbly dresser, which Beany despised so, and stretched to her utmost to hold the curtain up. Beany was almost smacking her lips, "Um-mm, it's simply golden—" when Mary Fred, stretching still farther to pull out a piece of ruffle, lost her balance. This thought zig-zagged swiftly through her mind as she went down, "If I hurt myself I'll have a good excuse for not going to the Formal."

But she didn't hurt herself. She only sat down with a thump on the part of her that was supposed to be sat on.

In the late afternoon the doorbell pealed demandingly, importantly. Mary Fred answered to find a special messenger having all he could do to balance two large gray garment boxes and hold out a paper which must be signed. "Miss Mary Fred Malone. Two specials. Sign here."

Even before she saw the contents of the boxes, Mary Fred's spirits stiffened with flattered excitement. *Miss Mary Fred Malone. Two specials. Bought by Mrs. Gaylord.*

Mary Fred opened the larger box first. From the folds of tissue paper she lifted something silken, and soft as down, yet weighty. The silkenness was the shell-pink lining of a coat which was folded fur side in.

Elizabeth was helping extract it from the encumbering tissue paper. She breathed out in awe, "It's one of those new blond fur evening coats. Coming here on the train I just happened to see one in a magazine I picked up. Oh yes, Mary Fred," as she reached out to stroke it while Mary Fred slid into it, "it's that new length. It mentioned it in the magazine, too—not quite as long as finger tip—thumb tip, they call it. It's luscious! Let's open the other box."

More knots to pull at impatiently, more tissue paper to pull back, more awed unbelief. This, too, seemed something that had magically stepped out of one of the ads in *Vogue*, something that belonged to the realm of the unattainable. The dress had a black lace bodice and a pale pink cloud of a skirt. There was sure sophistication in the way the dress was cut low to the waist in back, in the long, snug-fitting sleeves. Elizabeth's only comment was a whispered, "Oh my gosh— oh my golly!"

And it fitted perfectly. "But then I'm a perfect twelve," Mary Fred muttered admiringly of the picture in the mirror. She thought fleetingly of what this dress would do to the dresses the other girls would wear. Lila had said of, hers, "So simple and sweet. It's stinko." And this dress would make it that. This dress wouldn't give the red taffeta Janet was wearing a chance to be anything but what it was—a dress two years old cut down to Janet's five feet two. Even Alberta's dress, on which she had labored so hard and lovingly, would be a school-made dress that had been marked A plus —and that was all.

Oh, but this dress would do more than that! It wouldn't let its wearer feel a shrinking uneasiness of playing second fiddle. . . . Mary Fred hugged it to her in rapture.

She couldn't thank Nonna enough when she came hurrying in about dinnertime. Nonna said, "It isn't just what I wanted. I'd rather have had it more teen-age and demure, but shopping at such an eleventh hour I had to take what I could get. I want Hattie to fix your hair to go with the dress. Hattie, you remember the young girl whose family had that place on Long Island that I did over for them? You remember I pointed her out to you one night when I gave a reception? You remember how her hair was done?"

So after a dinner, which seemed to Mary Fred quite unnecessary, and after her bath, Hattie seated her before the dressing table and flicked a firm, deft comb through her dark brown hair. Mary Fred wore her hair, as did ninety per cent of the girls at Harkness High, with a casual pompadour on top and the rest falling into loose, uneven, curly lengths.

"You're good, Hattie," Mary Fred said, watching in the mirror as Hattie did things to her front and side hair that made it less sixteen-year-oldish, though she left the rest falling, tumbled and soft, to touch her shoulders. "You ought to be a hairdresser. You did start out to be one, didn't you?"

"I'd have been one," Hattie said dully, "if it hadn't been for Mrs. Gaylord." She was pulling a few tangled wisps of hair out of the comb. Very slowly she pulled them out, wound them around her finger, threw the hair spiral into the wastebasket. "I needed to get a little money ahead before I could go home and open my own parlor. So I went to work for Mrs. Gaylord. Then I had to have an operation. She was so good to me. She got the best doctors, she paid my hospital. It's hard to go against anyone who's done things for you."

"It isn't too late, is it, for you to go into beauty parlor work if you like it?"

Hattie said tiredly, "Year after year, year after year, I think I will break away and do for myself. Kindness makes slaves and weaklings of people so much easier than unkindness. . . . Here, I'll put your make-up on. Mrs. Gaylord thought you needed a darker make-up."

Hattie picked up the dress, slipped it carefully over Mary Fred's head. While she was pulling the skirt down Mary Fred straightened the lace sleeves, pulled up the zipper that made the black lace fit snug enough to show the cobweb design in it.

From the minute Mary Fred's head showed above that black lace which topped the diaphanous skirt that wasn't ordinary pink but a shell pink which was more of a glow than a color, she had an unreal feeling that she was someone else. Her hair didn't feel like Mary Fred's hair; her eyes didn't seem to look out of Mary Fred's face; her heart didn't seem to beat in Mary Fred's body.

She even turned at the door and looked back—at the saddle shoes with those dirty wrinkles across the instep, at the scarf frayed at the ends from much tying and untying over her head. And they seemed to belong to another girl. To a mop-squeezer. Not to this queen in a dress that was cocksure, even insolent. Certainly no one could say of this girl, "There's that poor kid Dike Williams gave a song and dance to, and then chucked overboard."

Elizabeth had been downstairs warming the fragrant oil for the baby's nightly rub. Elizabeth stared at her sister and laughed uneasily. "But, Mary Fred, where are *you?* You look like a twenty-year-old divorcee."

Mary Fred looked at her from a great height. How had she ever thought that Elizabeth was glamour plus? Elizabeth had never worn a dress that looked like something from a Hollywood premiere. Mary Fred said, "Did you notice how Hattie pinned the pink camellias across the back of my hair?" She picked up the soft weight of fur coat, descended the stairs.

Ander was waiting at the foot of the stairs. He held the fur evening coat for her, whistled low. "And here I was getting ready to pat you on the back and give you a word of cheer, thinking you'd be scared of what lay ahead."

"Not in this dress," she said. "I feel like a lady spy leading on her victim."

Ander sometimes said such strange things. "I'd like you better if you were a little scared."

It wasn't until the dance was over and the dress was hung in the closet and Mary Fred was in her striped butcher-boy pajamas, with one pocket almost ripped off, that she came back to herself. As she passed the pink-and-white bassinet, she peered in and saw it was empty. She whispered, "Elizabeth, where's the baby?"

Elizabeth jerked upright in bed. With her hair in two

soft pigtails, and her cheeks flushed with sleep, she looked young and like Beany. And in that sleepy moment, she muttered out the thoughts that must have been uppermost in her mind. "I wanted him on the chairs right here by the bed. And so I put him here. I bootlegged one of the nighties Don and I made and put it on him. He's my baby and Don's —and neither of us had anything to do with that fancy bassinet." Elizabeth snuggled back sleepily on her pillow, her hand groping toward the baby to be sure he was covered.

In her own bed on the porch Mary Fred stretched out. The fresh night wind blew across her face and she reached down and pulled the blanket at the foot of the bed up closer under her chin. As she lay there, the evening passed before her like pictures on a screen. She wasn't sure she liked the heroine, that flippant, head-high girl in a dress almost alarming in its sophisticated loveliness.

And the girl's arrogance had lived up to the dress. Ander said as he helped her into the car, "You might sit back there with Aunt Lucille." Mary Fred had felt a covert friendliness on the woman's part, as though she wanted to make a friendly overture. But the girl sat coolly aloof beside the woman who had referred to her as one of "the awful Malones."

Mary Fred's feet felt cold at the foot of the bed; she crooked her knees and pulled them into the warmer area. She went on watching the reel. Ander guiding the girl through the hotel lobby. The Spring Formal wasn't held at the school gym but in one of the hotel ballrooms downtown. Ander, for all he was from a Wyoming ranch, was equally at home in a city. He had gone two years to a university near Chicago.

He knew enough (some of the boys didn't) to stop at the

check stand. "We'll leave our wraps here." Only part of
Mary Fred's mind noted how his tux made him look—taller,
slimmer, and his ruddy features more clear-cut. Mary Fred
relived again the check girl's envious adulation as she folded
the blond fur coat, silken side out, and gave it a caressing
stroke before she put it on the shelf.

And then the dance, and the girl in the black lace so com-
placently sure of herself. She hadn't been very kind, that girl.
She hadn't cared because her dress made Lila's white dress
look junior-high. And when Alberta, in front of the powder-
room mirror, pulled worriedly at her cream lace dress and
said, "Look at the way the zipper bunches up," she could
have hunted a pin and done something about it. And when
Janet, the generous, said from her rustling red taffeta, "Mary
Fred, you'll knock 'em for a loop," why didn't she assure
her, "So will you, honey"? The old Mary Fred would have.

But this—this next part of the reel, Mary Fred in her
butcher-boy pajamas couldn't go over without her heart
thumping under the blankets. Dike Williams had claimed
every dance he could get with her. Dike had said, "Mary
Fred, you're a straight-arm stagger. What's happened to
you?"

"You'd be surprised."

"This fellow you came with—he hasn't edged me out of
the picture, has he?" The old Mary Fred, mop-squeezer,
would have been fool enough to have blurted right out, "Oh
no, he couldn't—he couldn't ever. Ander is just nice, but
you—you're de-gee."

But the girl in the black lace only laughed and said, "We'll
not talk about that."

And the dress had given her the insouciance to tell him
that he might as well drop her like a hot potato because

Martie Malone wasn't the kind to boost a football player on anything but football ability. Dike hadn't answered for a minute. She wondered if he might apologize, if he might deny that he was courting Coach Hibbs via Martie Malone via his daughter.

They were dancing and he finished the open, side-by-side steps. But when he swung her about and they danced off together, he said with his appealing smile, "Let's put that in the past, squaw. I'm the one who's worried about you dropping me. You've got me feverish. When I saw you come in the door tonight I fell for you. You're a queen—and smooth—and how!"

Dike hadn't dropped her like a hot potato. Far from it. He had cut in again. Dike's girl, Sylvia, had watched them. At school parties she had watched them with a complacency which Mary Fred knew now could be translated, "I needn't worry about Dike rushing Mary Fred Malone if it'll help him get to State U with me next year." But now she didn't look so serene.

No, the girl with the pink camellias in her hair hadn't been very kind. One of the refreshment committee had sought her out worriedly. "Mary Fred, the caterer is raising a holy rumpus. There're about seven sherbet cups that haven't been turned in. You know how they leave them sitting around just anywhere."

"Sorry, old dear, but I'm not going up and peer under every potted palm. Let someone else stew about them." And she had danced off with Dike Williams. She was through mop-squeezing while others queened.

Ander had fitted in nicely. The other girls came to Mary Fred with their enthusiasm. "Mary Fred, where have you been keeping this great strong man from the plains?" But to the girl who had eyes only for Dike Williams' black curly head, he was merely a tall quiet boy with eyes that were bluer and more thoughtful—sometimes more teasing—than most. He was only something there when you needed it— like the stirrups to press hard on in hurdle-jumping. And to think she had been so terrified of this hurdle!

Ander brought her home in his aunt's car. She had gone on from the concert with friends. At the front door Mary Fred had said—because in a dress that was all assuredness, you could say flip things and get away with them—"Well, did you suffer too terribly doing your good deed?"

She had been getting away with remarks like that all evening, but she didn't get away that time. "Pretty terribly," he admitted. He even went further, "You know, I could shake you, you little coot! If ever anybody worked hard at peacemaking between you folks and Aunt Lu, I have—"

"Here it comes," Mary Fred said brightly. "Aunt Lu's heart of gold beating under a diamond tiara."

"I soften her up by telling her what real folks you Malones are—"

"In our heathenish way, of course."

"—and I think to myself, 'Now everything will be hunky-dory. We'll go downtown together tonight and Aunt Lu will see that Mary Fred is a nice, well-meaning kid—'"

Nice, well-meaning kid! But Dike Williams had told her she was a straight-arm stagger. "I'm the one who's worried about you dropping me," he had said.

She answered Ander haughtily, "I'm through being a nice, well-meaning kid. What do they get, anyway?" He turned toward the door and because, somehow, she wanted him to say something complimentary about her dress, or her charm, or the hit she had made at the prom, she prodded further, "I'm sorry the evening was—well, such a total loss."

But still Ander wouldn't pay the girl in black lace tribute. "At least it was different. It's the first time I ever took a girl out who didn't wear the corsage I sent." He stifled a yawn, said goodnight, and was gone.

It was not until the next day that Mary Fred, opening the icebox to get the baby's lime water, discovered, still in their cellophane drum-shaped box, the white gardenias Ander had sent her. Hattie must have answered the door and put them there. But Nonna, having decided that pink camellias were the perfect complement of the new formal, had seen that Mary Fred wore pink camellias.

And Mary Fred couldn't be sorry the white gardenias had wasted their beauty and fragrance on the icebox. Because Dike had noticed the pale pink flowers in her hair. "Lady of the Camellias, eh?" he had smiled at her as they danced.

14

"What Is the Matter with Johnny?"

THE Monday after the dance, Mary Fred Malone walked up the steps of Harkness High a different girl. The strong potion of flattery and envy, mixed with Dike Williams' ardent attention, had worked a transformation. And, even as in the strange case of Dr. Jekyll and Mr. Hyde, she couldn't step back into the role of Mary Fred, mop-squeezer at Harkness, helper and leaner-on in the Malone home.

But there was no need for either a helper or a leaner-on in the Malone household now. For, under Nonna's capable hands, the house ran like a well-planned decorating business. The living room could have been the reception room for a lady decorator, with every cushion in plump position, with every vase of flowers a study in harmony.

"Growing children need gracious living," Nonna said again and again.

There was nothing casual or carefree in the evening meal at the Malones' now. Behind the silver service Nonna sat—not Beany, who used to stand up so as to peer into cups.

Hattie always appeared at exactly the right moment to remove the soup plates or pass hot rolls.

But over and over again, Beany waylaid Mary Fred to ask, "What is the matter with Johnny?"

"I didn't know anything was the matter with him. Why?"

"You don't ever hear him spout about the flood of '64, or the silver bricks they laid for General Grant to walk on. You don't ever hear him banging away on his typewriter."

"That new one doesn't make the ungodly clatter his old threshing machine did."

"There's something the matter with him. Have you noticed him eating biscuits? I mean *not* eating biscuits? You know how many he used to eat!" Johnny had a no-waste motion all his own in eating biscuits. He never had to take two hands to break one. He had a deft, breaking-apart movement with his left hand while his right held the butter knife ready. Mary Fred, taking mental inventory of the times Hattie had passed biscuits, realized that Johnny was indeed not up to par. Beany went on, "He even acts polite to me. There's something the matter with him."

"You just imagine it, Beany. Maybe it's because Nonna had him cut his hair and we don't have to keep telling him to push it out of his eyes."

"He glooms," said Beany positively.

And then Ander asked Mary Fred the same thing. "What's the matter with Johnny these days?" Mary Fred answered him even as she had Beany, "I didn't know there was anything the matter with him. Why?"

Ander asked, "Do you know if he's mad at me about anything? Or did I do anything to hurt him? I wouldn't hurt him—you know I think Johnny's the swellest egg." He grinned at her. "Or should I say egg in front of a Malone?"

Mary Fred laughed a little ruefully. "Nonna threw out all those eggs we were struggling with. And you know what Beany did? After all her raving about mangled eggs, Beany almost cried. And even Johnny, I think, will always carry about a frustrated something because he didn't get to try another Lady Eleanor cake."

Ander went back to his starting point. "But I can't figure out that mugwump of a Johnny. I was coming home from school day before yesterday in Aunt Lu's old car and I yelled and asked him if he wanted a ride. And he just shook his head and kept going. I've yelled at him a couple of times over at your house. The joe avoids me. He dodges me."

Mary Fred shook her head and changed the subject. "Ander, will you do something for me? I didn't have time to brush Mr. Chips last night and he ought to have it to-night, and will you do it for me?"

"I'll do it for Mr. Chips," he said readily. "The old mustang is coming along swell, isn't he? Another month and I don't think we'll have to worry about his leg. Did you rub that liniment in last night?"

"No—no, I didn't."

"You should have," he reproved her.

She wouldn't tell him that she was afraid that when Dike Williams danced with her he'd notice that her hair smelled like a stable. Once he had said something about it. So now she evaded, "I'm always breaking a finger nail when I'm a stable boy." She held out her hands; she had worked a full hour on her nails the previous evening. It was a new shade and Dike Williams had noticed that her lipstick was the same shade.

But of course Ander didn't. He only said, "You've got too much lipstick on, gal."

142

Ander worked about the garage-stable for hours that evening. He exercised Mr. Chips; he rubbed him down; he put in clean straw for bedding. Mary Fred saw his light burning later than usual as he caught up with his studying.

And still another person was to stop Mary Fred and ask her, "What is the matter with Johnny?"

It was Miss Hewlitt who called to Mary Fred as she passed the English Lit room at Harkness. Mary Fred dropped down on top of a desk and rested her books on her knees while she looked at Miss Hewlitt. Like Nonna, Miss Hewlitt gave an impression of grayness with her gray hair, gray eyes, and grayish clothes. But unlike Nonna, there was no cool luster of silver; hers was more of a soft tweed grayness, durable and worn and color-flecked.

Mary Fred repeated her question, "What is the matter with Johnny? That's getting to be a refrain—like that poem of Milne's:

"*What* is the matter with Mary Jane?
She hasn't an ache and she hasnt' a pain,
And it's lovely rice pudding for dinner again.
What *is* the matter with Mary Jane?"

Miss Hewlitt smiled wryly. "I'm not sure about Johnny not having an ache or pain—I mean in his soul, not his stomach. What about The Book, Mary Fred—our book, as we call it? They don't seem to be getting along on it, do they?"

"They're not exactly galloping along the way they did at first. But then Emerson Worth hasn't been out for quite a while."

"Why not?"

143

Mary Fred squirmed unhappily. She readjusted her books, sighed. "He and Nonna don't seem to vibrate. She thinks he's a maundering old crackpot."

"He's a historical genius," snapped Miss Hewlitt. Her voice slowed with her fondness for Johnny, her understanding of him. "That accounts for Johnny's restless unhappiness. Because that book was pounding through his veins. It's cruel to keep him and old Emerson from working together. They each need the other so."

She sat at her desk, tapping thoughtfully with her pencil. "But there's something else the matter with Johnny, Mary Fred. What gives him that hangdog look?"

"I don't know," Mary Fred said soberly. "I just don't know."

Miss Hewlitt hesitated a moment before she asked, "Mary Fred, hasn't something happened to you, too?"

Mary Fred didn't answer. The answer would have been, "I'm a queen, not a mop-squeezer. Dike Williams is the star forward on the basketball team—and I'm his girl." But what sense would that make to a gray-haired English Lit teacher who thought the perfect evening's entertainment was reading Chaucer.

Miss Hewlitt said, "I've always loved you Malones. I taught your father and he was so honest, so unshirking. And so are you children. I've always thought you Malones were more blessed than other families. You children have a father you can be proud of; and your father has children he can be proud of. It doesn't always work that way."

Mary Fred felt baffled, uneasy. She flung out, even as she had that day to Beany, "Father's proud of Elizabeth—she's so lovely; and of Johnny—Johnny's so brilliant; and of Beany—Beany's so capable. But I—I'm not so *anything*."

And Miss Hewlitt said almost the same thing Beany had said. "Mary Fred, you're the ballast of the Malone family. They all turn to you." She added soberly, "Don't fail them, Mary Fred."

As Mary Fred walked up their front-porch steps that afternoon, Elizabeth came to the door, waving a letter.

"From Don?" Mary Fred asked eagerly, knowing how anxiously Elizabeth was awaiting word from him.

"No, from Father—from Hawaii."

Like all Father's letters, it was scribbled with a soft pencil on copy paper. He had sent messages to each one. "Mary Fred and Elizabeth, please keep our home open for any fun you can give the soldiers. They need that friendly pat on the back." To Beany: "Here's a recipe for you. I can't spell the Hawaiian but it means 'Rice and Eggs.'" And lastly, "Johnny, be sure you put in your book about Eugene Field and his poems and paragraphs and practical jokes when he worked on the paper in the early days. Get Emerson to tell you about the time he impersonated Oscar Wilde—with his auburn wig, and bright-colored cravat, and carrying a lily. I think about The Book a lot, Son, and what a chance it'll be for you both."

Johnny came in, tramped up to his room. Ordinarily Johnny routed his way through the house past the icebox. But not of late. Mary Fred followed him to his room with the letter.

He was sitting with his long legs stretched out on the blue chipped desk. The cover was pulled neatly over the typewriter. When had a typewriter in Johnny's room had a cover on it?

Mary Fred read him Father's message. Johnny said, "Yes, I remember hearing about Eugene Field impersonat-

145

ing the Disciple of the Beautiful. How the Welcome Committee met him and drove him through the streets and all the crowd bowing and cheering." But there was no bounce in his voice, no eagerness in his fingers to get it on paper.

Mary Fred asked, "Johnny, what *is* the matter with you?"

"What's the matter with me—why?"

"That's what everyone is asking me. Ander thinks you're mad at him or that he did something to hurt you. He says you dodge him."

Johnny's feet came down off the desk with a bang. He walked to the window and back again. He said miserably, "I'm ashamed—that's why, Sis. I guess by now Mrs. Thompson, the egg woman on their ranch, has told him about coming here—and about my going back on my word. Ander must think I'm a heel."

"You went back on your word? Why, Johnny Malone, you never in your life went back on your word! You're too— too conscientious."

Johnny faced her, and the unhappiness in his thin face stabbed at her heart. "That's what she said—Nonna—that there was such a thing as being too conscientious. Of course, I know Nonna thought she was doing me a favor. And she's been good to me—getting me this brand new typewriter. And I don't know—I'm all mixed up."

Mrs. Thompson, Mary Fred gathered from his account, had come on her monthly trip to the dentist and for her monthly collecting from Johnny to pay on the bashed fender and front light. But Nonna had talked to her. She had made it clear to Mrs. Thompson that her claim would never hold up in court. Of course, it was regrettable, but in an accident both parties must accept some loss. Johnny had already paid a good share of the damage, besides taking those worthless eggs off her hands, and she, Nonna, felt the whole incident should be closed.

Mary Fred could picture it so clearly. Mrs. Thompson, ill at ease, frightened even, holding her hand to her mouth where a pulled tooth had left a gap. Mary Fred could imagine her edging out the door which Nonna closed decisively behind her.

Johnny appealed to her. "What do you think I ought to do, Mary Fred?"

Miss Hewlitt had said, "They all turn to you." But Mary Fred, remembering the lace formal, the fur evening wrap, the green flannel jacket, remembering the hours of drudgery Nonna spared her, couldn't help but defend her. "I'd skip it, Johnny. In one way she's right, Nonna is, you have paid plenty."

"But I told Mrs. Thompson I would. Ander stood up for me against the policeman because he said he knew my word would be as good as the policeman's record to hold over me. I feel so skunky."

The mailman always came down Barberry Street just about the time Mary Fred parted from Lila at her corner and came on home. And always Elizabeth, with the spring wind ruffling her skirts and her light hair, would be watching for him.

Often when Mary Fred came up, Elizabeth would be standing, sorting through the mail with listless hands and trying to pretend that her eyes were red because the wind had blown something in them. Or sometimes she couldn't pretend. When Mary Fred would ask, "Didn't you hear from Don yet?" her voice would choke out, "No—no, not yet." And Mary Fred would slide her arm around her and feel the tremors of held-back sobs in Elizabeth's slim body.

Yet Elizabeth put her anxiety behind her and always matched Lila's enthusiasm for entertaining the soldiers. Elizabeth and Lila and Ander had planned to have square dances regularly at the Malones'. The living room and dining room could accommodate four sets. Elizabeth had found a girl, a student at the university, who could play the accordion. Ander could call the dances. And they could serve doughnuts and coffee. "Or milk," Lila put in, because Private Clancy drank milk.

But always Nonna had a reason why they could not have their square-dance party. Either she planned for Hattie to wax the floors that day or she had invited other guests. And twice Nonna had a headache and couldn't stand the noise.

15

"Goodbye, Mr. Chips!"

MARCH was ending now and the days had the feel of spring to them. Mary Fred had always loved the feeling of things happening in the soil, and life quickening in the stark naked trees. She loved the newness, the gentle excitement of spring.

But spring this year meant clothes, and dates—and Dike —oh, especially Dike. Dike, who was winning the basketball championship for Harkness with his unerring aim in shooting baskets! Dike, the idol of Harkness!

She was walking home with Dike Williams this day and, as always when she was with Dike, everything else fell into the background. While they lingered at the Malone gate, Dike was telling her that there was talk of a party to be held for the team and their dates after the game this evening. If it materialized, he would let her know.

She resented Ander's coming down the street and interrupting them, for Dike went hurrying off. Ander was carrying something that looked like a huge gray cube of domino sugar. "Salt," he explained to Mary Fred. "You didn't get any for Chips, did you?"

"No, I didn't."

"I was afraid you'd keep forgetting it, so when I was at the ranch Sunday I picked up a chunk."

They walked down the driveway together. Nonna must be having company, for a car sat in the driveway. A workman with a push broom and a wheelbarrow was just finishing cleaning the garage. Mary Fred looked into the garage, looked amazedly at Ander. There was no sign of a horse or of a horse's surroundings in the roomy garage. The workman was sweeping up the last clutter of straw. The smell of smoke was in the air; it came from a pile of straw which was smouldering to a black heap.

Mary Fred asked, "Where is Mr. Chips?"

"I ain't seen no Mr. Chips. It was the lady that—"

"I mean the horse—the black horse?"

"I don't know a thing about a horse. I just know he was took away. She had me clean all this up. Said she didn't want a lot of smells and flies around with nice weather coming on."

Nonna came out of the house with her guests, walked to the car with them, waved goodbye. She faced the young folks and warded off Mary Fred's question before she could ask it. "I guess you're surprised, aren't you? I knew it would be a shock, but it's much better this way. We can't help but form an attachment to any animal we have around us, and that always dulls the real issue."

"What did you do with him?" Ander asked.

"I sent him where he'll get perfect care. I could see what an awful burden he was for you, Mary Fred. And such a responsibility! What kind of a place was this for a horse?

My dear, I'm surprised that your father gave in to you and ever let you bring him home. It was all a foolish mistake."

Mary Fred said, "But I—I hadn't finished paying for him yet. I still owed Mack—let's see, fifteen dollars less the six I paid him."

Ander asked bluntly, "Did you sell Mr. Chips? How could you when Mary Fred hadn't finished her deal with Mack?"

Nonna said, "You needn't worry about that, either of you. I'm a businesswoman. I settled with Mack, so that I could get a clear bill of sale."

Mary Fred said, "But Mr. Chips wasn't all well—not yet."

"My dear child, I took care of everything. I had a veterinary out and he said he was sound as a dollar. He'll be much better off at a stable."

"What stable did you sell him to?" Mary Fred asked.

Nonna didn't answer. She turned toward the house. "The wind is chilly without a wrap. Come on in, you two, and have a cup of tea. Hattie's got dozens of little sandwiches—one-biters, as your Johnny calls them." She laughed her silvery, soft laugh and hurried on into the house.

Ander looked in no mood for tea. He said grimly, "Mr. Chips wasn't as sound as a dollar! No reliable stable would buy him. You know what some of these stables are. They're horse-killers. All they care about is the seventy-five cents an hour they can rent a horse for. When Mr. Chips goes lame on them, they'll get rid of him to a glue factory or one of these fox farms as food for the foxes."

Mary Fred stood in wretched indecision without answering. She heard their gate click and she turned to see who was coming in. The front entrance of the Malone house faced on the driveway at the side. The gate had clicked behind old Emerson Worth and he came up the walk with his shaky-legged strut. The front steps onto the porch slowed both his legs and his strut. What a shabby, helpless, chilled old man he was! Mary Fred could almost hear her father say, "He needs hot coffee and bracing up."

Yet it was with dreary annoyance that Mary Fred planned in her mind, "I'll go in the back way. If Nonna's had a party there'll be coffee I can heat. I'll get the coffee down him and then Johnny can take him over. He needs Johnny's interest and their working together even more than he does the coffee."

Ander, too, was watching the old man. He gave a short laugh and said, "Evidently he wasn't invited in." For Emerson Worth turned from the door and stumbled back down the steps. He saw Mary Fred and Ander and bent his steps toward them.

Mary Fred reached out to steady the old man. He dropped down on the garden bench. His smile flickered mockingly through the deep wrinkles of his face. "I never noticed before what a solid front door you had. And how firmly it shuts."

Beany came down the back steps of the house with a cup of steaming coffee. She looked both secretive and defiant. "Here, Emerson, drink this," she urged.

"He'd better go inside," Mary Fred said. "The wind *is* sharp."

"*She* didn't want him in," Beany imparted.

Emerson Worth made a grand oratorical gesture. "Martie Malone flies to Hawaii in the cause of democracy, and his home has been taken over by the dictator. Have you Malones learned the salute yet?"

Mary Fred defended, "She's bought us all such lovely things."

Of course, that was the wrong thing to say to old Emerson Worth. Of course, that brought forth from Emerson Worth the quotation that made Mary Fred groan inwardly, " 'The highest price you can pay—' "

The workman interrupted. He had piled into a carton Mr. Chips' brushes and currycombs, the bottles of liniment, the bandage wrapping, the saddle soap. He was looking indeterminedly toward the smouldering bonfire. "She told me to get rid of everything."

The bridle and halter and saddle and blanket must have gone with the horse. When this carton was gone there would be nothing left of the black horse that had nickered with such glad excitement every time Mary Fred opened the door.

Ander said roughly, "Those don't go on the bonfire. Give them here. I'll take them home." He turned to Mary Fred and his voice was still rough. "You've got to find out where your Nonna sold Mr. Chips. You aren't going to let her get away with that, are you?"

Mary Fred said miserably, "I hate to make a scene about it. She's done so many nice things for us. I guess she did think Mr. Chips was a lot of trouble and expense for all of us. I think he'll be all right."

"You don't think it at all," he flung at her. "You're letting Nonna do your thinking for you. Don't you care? Or is it easier to be a clothes rack and let Nonna do your caring for you?"

She retorted angrily, "Stop being so bossy. After all, it's our business. You're like your aunt, Mrs. Socially-Prominent Adams—so opinionated and superior!"

She thought for part of a minute he was going to shake her. He took an exasperated, driven step toward her. Just then Hattie called from the kitchen doorway, "Mary Fred —telephone. Said to tell you it was Dike Williams."

That was all Mary Fred needed and immediately everything else receded into dim background. Emerson Worth sitting there on the bench drinking Beany's coffee, Nonna's disposal of Mr. Chips, and her own angry quarrel with Ander who had always been there when she needed him.

She ran into the house. Dike Williams' voice over the telephone and Mary Fred's heart doing a rat-a-tat under her yellow sweater! "Look, squaw, the party after the game is cinched. So wear the glad rags. I'll be by for you. Coach wants us down early."

Mary Fred hung up the telephone. She'd get Hattie to do her hair. She'd wear that dark tropical make-up. The girls who came with the players always sat in the front seats of the gym. They always held the bulky sweat shirts the team wore while warming up and between halves. She could feel Dike Williams tossing her his when the whistle blew. She would stand up to catch it, thus proclaiming herself his choice. People in the grandstand would nudge each other and say, "That's Dike Williams' girl. The one in the green coat. They go everywhere together."

16

A Border of Angels

THE MALONES, with the exception of Elizabeth, were at
school during the day so that they never saw the machina-
tions of Nonna. They saw only the results. Her plans always carried so perfectly. Elizabeth said, "It's unbeliev-
able—it's uncanny the way she puts things through. She
can sit at the telephone for an hour and have more people
talked into doing more things."

It was on Monday when Mary Fred, returning from
school, found that Mr. Chips was gone from Barberry
Street. Any loss she felt over his going, and her quarrel
with Ander, was glossed over by all the rush and feting of
the successful basketball team, and her sharing it all by going with Dike Williams.

On Wednesday when Mary Fred came home a furniture
truck was backed up to their side door. As she came into
the hall two men in white overalls were coming down the
stairs. One was carrying a ladder and the other paper-
hanging tools.

From the head of the stairs Nonna cried out, "Oh my dear, you frightened me for a minute! I was afraid it was Beany, and I didn't want her to see her room until it was quite finished. We would have been through if the furniture had only arrived when they promised it."

"Beany will be here any minute now," Mary Fred said. "She's only a few minutes behind me usually."

"But not this afternoon," Nonna smiled. "I saw to it that she would be delayed." Nonna always saw to such details. She had asked the mother of one of Beany's friends to take Beany downtown shopping with her and her young daughter. Beany would be later than usual arriving home.

Mary Fred went up to Beany's room. Nonna was telling the men where to put the two new pieces of furniture—a bed and a dresser of some modern bleached wood. Hattie had just finished washing the window for which Beany was making yellow-plaid curtains. But Hattie and Nonna were lifting a pair of curtains which had come from the decorating department of a downtown store.

"The bedspread matches," Nonna said, as she handed the curtain rod with its billowy green skirts to Hattie. Curtains and bedspread were of a sheer, yet silken, chartreuse material. "Aren't they delicious with the bleached wood furniture?" Nonna commented.

But it was at the walls that Mary Fred stared. "They're pink," she said aloud.

"Desert coral," Nonna corrected her. "And just to add the ingénue touch, which one mustn't overlook in a young girl's room, I chose that border." Mary Fred's eyes lifted to the border of roses which fell into scallops and was held up by chubby, smiling cherubs.

Mary Fred said, "The room is—is beautiful." But she and Elizabeth looked at each other with mixed feelings. They went to work putting Beany's clothes back into the closet, laying her blouses and underthings in the drawers of the new dresser. Hattie cleaned the rug with the vacuum cleaner, while Nonna smoothed the billowy chartreuse spread on the bed.

It was an exotic, even seductive, room. Beany's plaid jumpers, her worn tennis shoes, her box of marbles, her smudgy recipe books seemed out of place.

Hattie was putting the sweeper away; Mary Fred was running the oiled mop around the dusty edges of the room; and Nonna was saying to Elizabeth, who was putting Beany's blue comb and brush set on the dresser, "No, no, don't put those out, they're a jarring note"—when Beany came.

She came tearing up the stairs as usual to look at the little mister. Elizabeth said to her gently as though she were breaking dubious news to her, "Beany, Nonna had your room done all over for you—for a surprise."

Certainly it was a surprise. Beany's round flushed face went lax as she stood in the doorway of her room. She stood and stared stupidly. She was breathing hard for she must have thought the baby would miss her if she didn't hurry home—and the consternation in her honest face twisted Mary Fred's heart.

"Isn't it gorgeous?" Nonna asked.

"Yes—it's gorgeous," Beany admitted.

Nonna went on proudly, "I used this same color scheme for a young debutante in Philadelphia. I'll never forget her face when she first saw it."

And I'll never forget Beany's, Mary Fred was thinking.

Nonna lifted the chartreuse curtains, the better to show their sheerness. Beany said, "I never saw curtains before that—that sort of bile green."

"Chartreuse," Nonna corrected. "And look at the wall. I lay awake the other night visualizing this room and I saw the chartreuse at the window and on the bed, and the soft coral of the wall, but I wasn't content. It hadn't the right touch and I knew it hadn't. So I went down yesterday to the wallpaper store and the minute I saw that rose-garland border with the angels I knew it was *jeune fille* and, at the same time, sophisticated. Look at the wall, Beany."

Beany was looking at the wall. She said in a small voice, "It said in the magazine that borders in a small room were oppressive—and they are. Those rabbits—I just thought I couldn't stand seeing them the last thing at night and the first thing in the morning."

Nonna passed that off. "I doubt if it was the rabbits, my dear. I think you eat too heartily in the evening."

Mary Fred winced again. She knew that Beany came home from school hollow as a reed because she saved the lunch money Nonna gave her for the mahogany stain she planned to use on her bed and the unfinished chest of drawers she wanted.

"And now," said Nonna, "we can leave this door open into the hall. We'll have guests Easter and we needn't feel ashamed of this horrid little hole."

Hattie called to Nonna then. The paper hangers wanted to ask her about the left-over rolls of paper, and Nonna went down.

Mary Fred reproached Beany, "You should have said you liked it. Land of love, you never even said 'thank you' after all the trouble she went to, trying to please you."

"She didn't do it to please me. If she had she'd have let me do the room the way I wanted. I wanted a wall that was halfway between robin's egg blue and the blue of the Madonna's robe."

"Oh, Beany dear," Elizabeth said, "maybe when you get used to these walls—these desert coral ones—you'll like them."

"I hate them. I hate those angels—" And suddenly Beany put her head against the woodwork of the door and sobbed, "I don't want fat angels looking down at me all the time. I'd sooner have rabbits. Does she think we can like things just because she thinks we ought? Does she think we can— feel—" sobs twisted the words, "the way—*she* thinks we— ought?"

Elizabeth patted her racking shoulders. "Oh, Beany— Beany, blessed, don't cry!" The baby was fussing in his bassinet. Elizabeth absently pushed the bassinet back and forth. She said, "I wonder if we Malones oughtn't to take a stand for what we've alway stood for. I wish I had more strength to go against her—I mean inner strength. But I haven't. I'm so worried about Don—" her own voice threatened to break and she took a second or two to straighten it out. "I don't seem to have enough energy or thought left over."

Beany was trying desperately to snuffle back her sobs. Elizabeth turned to Mary Fred appealingly. "Mary Fred, weren't we truer to our ideals? Oh, now that sounds like a political speech, but I mean, weren't we really *us* when we were on our own feet, before Nonna came and did all the providing and deciding for us?"

Beany lifted her tear-streaked face. "She buys us by giving us things," she said with swollen lips. "It never made sense before what old Emerson Worth was always saying—about the highest price you could pay for something was to get it for nothing. Look at Johnny! He's never home any more. He's always over at Carlton's. He never uses his new typewriter. It was like music to hear Johnny pounding that old one. I'm so—so homesick for *us*—the way we used to be."

Elizabeth said slowly, "I don't like myself for taking the clothes Nonna buys me. They seem to come between Don and me, and the dreams we dreamed. I felt better *inside* when I was denying myself things that Don and I couldn't afford." She entreated, "Oh, Mary Fred, you're the strong one of the Malones. You help us get back to our old way— even if Nonna is here. You—you kind of lead us, won't you?"

"Just like I said," Beany said thickly, "you're the leaner-on, Mary Fred."

The old way! But Mary Fred could only remember Dike Williams telephoning for a date and her hands and her apron—even her spirit—soapsudsy with doing the Saturday washing. She remembered mornings so busy she scarcely had time to do her hair, much less her nails. And then having to hurry home from school to get dinner started. And Mr. Chips, out in the garage, eating up every extra nickel she could earn.

But since Nonna came, there had been no worry over finances, no work. There had been time for loitering happily along with Dike, time for every party Dike asked her to. She had had clothes to startle Dike's crowd.

She said harshly, "I can see that the old way was dog-goned hard. We made such fool mistakes and then suffered for them. We went off to school looking like lumps. If

Nonna wants to do things for us in her own way, I think we're silly to get hysterical just because Beany doesn't like the angels on her wall."

April arrived with bright assurance that now at last winter had blustered his way out and spring had come smiling in. Jonquils and hyacinths shot out of the ground and showed new and untouched against the drab brick and weather-beaten stone of houses. The weeping willow in the Malone back yard draped itself in yellow-green lace.

Easter was the first Sunday in April, and following Easter was a week of spring vacation. Nonna was making plans for Easter. She would give an Easter breakfast, buffet style, for many of her friends. "It seems regrettable," Nonna said, "that your father didn't see that you young people met the worth-while people in the town."

Johnny said, "We always have Emerson Worth out for Easter because he doesn't have anyone belonging to him."

Nonna said gently, "I'm afraid he wouldn't enjoy himself with the group I'm having. He wouldn't fit in at all."

Plans for Easter touched Mary Fred with an uneasy remembering. The last time Jock and Lorna had been at the house, she had promised them that they should come and help her and Beany dye Easter eggs. She remembered how avidly—though Jock pretended male indifference—they had soaked up her talk about the Easter rabbit leaving baskets filled with colored and candy eggs.

But Mary Fred had never mentioned it since, so surely they weren't counting on it. The youngsters would only clutter up the Easter they were planning now. Church in

the morning, of course, and then Nonna's Easter breakfast
at noon. But that wasn't the highlight of the day. Dike
Williams and his crowd were driving up to a mountain
lodge in the late afternoon. They'd have a trout supper
there in the rustic dining room. They'd play the victrola
and sing, dance a little perhaps, and watch the moon lift
over the mountain peaks.

As day followed day, Elizabeth's eyes grew heavier,
dark-circled with sleepless anxiety. She spent hours with
her eyes watching the street where the mailman turned. But
no word had come to her from Lieutenant Donald Mac-
Callin.

The Saturday before Easter was a gray, drizzly day.
Mary Fred went over to Lila's, and they spent the morning
making cookies for the Soldiers' Recreation Center. Lila
and she drove through a misty rain to deliver them.

Lila's day was quite complete because she saw Private
Clancy—more than complete because he showed her the
stripe on his sleeve which told the world he was now Private
First Class Clancy. They sat there in the midst of the chat-
ter over checker games, a lackadaisical fingering of piano
keys, the click of billiard balls, and smiled into each other's
eyes. "He asked about Elizabeth's baby," Lila relayed happily to Mary Fred.

And while Mary Fred was at the Center, the hostess
asked her if she would help her pack a record a soldier had
made to send to his folks at home. "It's a service we have
for the soldiers," the woman explained. "They come in
here and talk a record off for their folks. That way the
home folks get to hear their voices." Mary Fred thought
fleetingly of Elizabeth and how precious a letter on a record
in Don's voice would be to her right now.

The hostess was saying as she placed the record on the machine, "We have to listen to it, and then sign the necessary papers when we mail it. Here's the name. Fill out this blank, Mary Fred."

The record had been made by one of Clancy's buddies. Mary Fred remembered dancing with him at the square dance the night Ander had called them. The record was playing. He was telling his folks the usual things—about early morning classes, bed-check, mess. Then Mary Fred quickened to hear their name mentioned.

> We've met the nicest folks named Malone. I enjoy going there like everything. Clancy took me around there. They promised us they'd have a dance for us at their house. I hope it'll be soon now. We get homesick to see the inside of a house and drink coffee that isn't made in fifty-gallon lots.

The hostess smiled at Mary Fred. "That's right, too. We do what we can for the fellows down here, but it isn't a home. That's what they're hungry for."

Mary Fred spoke out of remorseful pangs. "We'll have that hoe-down real soon for them." But she couldn't feel sure that they would. Nonna didn't like the idea of twelve or sixteen soldiers taking the wax polish off the floors as they swung on the corner, and promenaded left.

17

Discipline

LILA and Mary Fred stopped at the neighborhood grocery on their way home from the Recreation Center. Both of them had lists which they drew from damp pockets.

On Mary Fred's list, which Nonna had made out in detail, was the item, "Five two-pound broilers." But the butcher had no broilers that small. "Better take two or three of these larger ones and you'll have the same amount of chicken," he advised.

Mary Fred said irresolutely, "I'll have to call Nonna and ask her."

Lila turned from the bread counter and looked at her aghast. "Mary Fred, surely you won't! I never thought one of you Malones couldn't decide for yourselves. I thought I was the only suppressed personality—as Janet says."

Mary Fred felt aghast at herself. And yet she didn't dare *not* call Nonna. She could hear her say in her gentle, yet firm voice, "My dear, when I put down one-pound broilers, I mean just that."

So Mary Fred telephoned home and Nonna said, "No, I don't want large ones—they don't broil so nicely. I'll get them myself downtown. I have to run down on some errands. Hurry on home, Mary Fred, I want you to make out the place cards for our breakfast tomorrow."

Lila let her out in front of her house. Ander was in Mrs. Adams' yard and he called to Mary Fred as though he had been watching for her. Since their quarrel they had given only the briefest of greetings, but now he came toward her. His face, under his damply glistening hair, wasn't friendly but was set in tight-jawed grimness. He nodded toward his aunt's car and said, "I want you to come with me. I want to show you something."

"I haven't got time. Nonna wants me to fix the place cards for our Easter breakfast party."

He took her arm peremptorily. "The place cards can wait a few minutes. This won't take long." He helped her into the front seat.

He drove, without speaking, down the road that edged the town and came to a riding stable which advertised, "Ride for enjoyment any time of day or night. Fast horses always available."

Across the road from the stables a man was plowing a field with an old-fashioned plow with one horse hitched to it. "That's what I wanted you to see," Ander said grimly.

Mary Fred looked at the horse plodding through the gray drizzle and her heart sank heavily, a deep pain inside her. She started to cry out, "That can't be Mr. Chips!" But she knew it was—knew by his limping walk and the splash of white in his forehead. The fallen star in his forehead! But those were the only similarities to the high-headed, smooth-limbed Mr. Chips that this plodding, heavy-headed horse bore. He slowed once, his slender hoofs sinking deep in the soft, wet earth. They heard the sharp crack of leather against his hide as the man urged him on.

Mary Fred cried out strickenly, "You're mean, Ander— you're mean, to bring me here and show me and—gloat over me!"

"I didn't bring you here to gloat over you," he said quietly, as he swerved the car around and started home. "I wanted you to see for yourself. You're always talking about Nonna and her being like a fairy godmother. I'm not up on my fairy tales but it seems to me I read about some old woman who fed a girl a poisoned apple and it stuck in her throat and she lay in a coma until something jolted her and it fell out. I wanted to jolt you."

Mary Fred sat beside him with a sick heart. She was helpless. For how could she get Mr. Chips back? If only Father were here—but he was thousands of miles away. He had given her a chance to buy Mr. Chips and she had let the chance fall through her fingers. Nonna had said she would get them anything they wanted. But it had to be something she wanted them to want.

Ander let her out at her gate without a word. Red walked out to meet her. The dog seemed as troubled and dejected as she, as he slumped beside her with no wag to his wet bushy tail.

Automatically Mary Fred opened the front door quietly. They had become used to doing that in case the baby was asleep. She leaned against the door jamb and shivered sickly.

The house seemed very quiet, almost deserted, except for the small fussing of the baby. He fussed this time of day because this was the time Beany usually took him for a ride in their old baby buggy. Mary Fred heard Nonna's voice

166

trying to quiet him. But Nonna, as she often admitted, was no hand with babies.

The thump of the iron in the kitchen explained why Nonna was with the baby instead of Hattie. Hattie was ironing—probably some of Nonna's finery for Easter. But where was Elizabeth? Where was Beany? And oh, it seemed strange not to have Johnny appear suddenly at the head of the stairs and yell down, "Hey, chunk, come on up here and read what I wrote."

Then one of Mary Fred's mental questions was answered. Mary Fred heard Nonna go to the door of Beany's room which opened off the hall at the head of the stairs. She heard something one seldom heard in the Malone home—the scrape of a key in a keyhole, the turning of it in the lock. Mary Fred heard the crispness in Nonna's voice as she said, "Beany, you may come out now."

Queer, unbelieving horror trickled through Mary Fred as she climbed the stairs. She said, "Nonna, you wouldn't lock Beany in her room! You *wouldn't!*"

But very evidently Nonna would. A stony-faced Beany came to the door. Nonna said, "I think you've had plenty of time to think over your ungratefulness and your obstinacy." Beany didn't answer. "Have you changed your mind about disfiguring the room I made so lovely for you?"

"No," Beany said.

Mary Fred looked beyond Beany into her room. Strips of paper, such as one uses on pantry or cupboard shelves, had been stretched over the border of roses and angels on the wall which faced Beany's bed. The paper was held in place by safety pins and tacks. Beany had taken down the "bile-green" curtains and hung up her one yellow-plaid gingham one.

"You can come out now," Nonna's firm voice went on. "I don't know what is keeping Elizabeth. I can't wait any longer. I have some errands downtown. I've called a cab."

Beany said bluntly, "You mean you're letting me out so I can take care of the baby. Mary Fred is home now, if you want to lock me up again."

Nonna didn't answer that. She had a habit of letting a question go unnoticed if she didn't feel it merited an answer. Instead she said to Mary Fred, "Do something a bit original with the place cards, won't you?"

"I'm not very original," Mary Fred said dully. She felt shaken and sick at the sight of Beany's tight, wretched face.

"Get Johnny in. He's been thumping around outside the house like a lost soul. He's good at thinking up things."

"Not any more he isn't," Mary Fred murmured. She wanted to scream out at Nonna, "Not since you separated him and old Emerson. They need each other. Miss Hewlitt said this book of theirs was pounding in Johnny's veins— and you stopped it. And besides you make Johnny ashamed inside by not letting him pay his just debts. He's so honorable, Johnny is. No wonder Miss Hewlitt is grieving about our Johnny."

Nonna was in her room putting on her hat and coat. She came out, pulling on a transparent rain cape, fitting the roomy hood of it over her small trim hat. She was like a beautiful, capable fashion plate, all wrapped in cellophane.

The cabdriver rang the front-door bell. Nonna turned at the top step to say to Beany, "I'm sure that when you think things over you'll realize how silly you're acting to make your room into the gruesome mess you have. I'm sure you'll fix it up as it should be."

"I don't like the fat angels," Beany said stubbornly.

"If the room isn't the way it should be in the morning, you'll spend all day Easter in it—in meditation."

Mary Fred cried out, "No Nonna, you can't do that—not to Beany—not on Easter Sunday. We're all going together to mass at St. Clara's Orphanage at nine o'clock. We always do. We always take the smallest children baskets of eggs."

Nonna said in that velvety tone of hers, only now Mary Fred felt the iron under it, "If Beany doesn't know obedience, then it's time it was taught her." And Nonna's high heels clicked down the stairs and out the front door to the waiting taxi.

The two girls stood there in the upstairs hall—shamed, somehow, and overcome. Then Beany, walking stiffly as though something had been broken inside her, went over to the whimpering baby. She had to swallow down a sob before she said, "Even if it is raining, I can wheel him up and down the porch. The nurse at St. Joseph's said fresh air wouldn't ever hurt them." Another sob, like a huge hiccough, quivered through her.

Mary Fred turned and fled down the back steps. A gusty rain peppered her face as she splashed across their yard. Red, wetly shining, looked up questioningly, hopefully, as he clung close to her. She leaped the hedge that separated their grounds from Mrs. Adams', went around the lily pool. Ander was on the sheltered back step. He was holding Tiffin and dabbing a piece of cotton, brown with iodine, on his soft flap of ear.

Mary Fred cried out, "Ander, it's been jolted out—the poisoned apple. I'm not in a coma now. Only I'm—honest, Ander, I'm scared of Nonna. She doesn't fight in the open. She has such a way of making us do what she wants. What can we do? Do you suppose we could write and tell Father and have him come home?"

Ander put Tiffin down and, for the first time, Tiffin didn't bark at Mary Fred. The little dog stood at her feet and looked up at her out of velvety brown eyes. Ander answered, "No, you can't send for your father, Mary Fred. You'll all just have to pool your strength and stand against her."

Mrs. Adams came to the door. She looked at Mary Fred's troubled face, and said quite naturally, "Come on in, child, out of the rain."

Even in her sharp misery, Mary Fred thought, "Ander's right, she is nice. Maybe from now on we'll be friends." And it warmed her chill fright to think that.

Ander said, "No, Aunt Lu, Mary Fred and I are just standing here plotting. . . . There's Elizabeth!"

Elizabeth must have got off the street car at the corner for she was coming down the sidewalk. The rain could no more dim Elizabeth's radiance than it could the red tulips in Mrs. Adams' tulip bed. Mary Fred and Ander ran and joined her as she reached the Malone gate. Elizabeth called as they scurried for the shelter of the porch, "Johnny, you come too. I want to tell you all something."

Johnny came from the vicinity of the garage. Beany was already on the porch; she was holding the baby, wondering if she should put him in the buggy with the rain drumming so loudly on the porch roof and splashing out of the rain spouts. Elizabeth took off her felt hat, and while she was shaking the rain drops off it she made glad announcement to them all, "I heard from Don. I got the letter this morning. And he sent me some money. That's why I went hurrying downtown to buy you all Easter baskets."

Red took this moment to shake himself and shower them all, but Elizabeth only laughed infectiously. She reached over and pulled Johnny's ear—it had the same tender affection as a kiss—and she pushed a bill into his hand. "And there's the money you spent for the little mister's clothes that first night I arrived."

Johnny said, "But it isn't mine. It was housekeeping money."

"You keep it, Johnny," Mary Fred said, and Beany echoed it, "You keep it."

Johnny looked down at the money and hope pushed through the wet sag of his figure. He asked, "Beany, how much did Mrs. Thompson say it cost her to get the fender ironed out and the light fixed?"

"Sixteen dollars—and thirty-two cents tax."

"And if I paid her five, how much do I still owe her?"

"Eleven thirty-two."

"I'll pay her this," Johnny said happily. "Oh gosh, but it's swell to know I can pay her."

Mary Fred said, "Elizabeth, now that you've heard from Don, do you feel strong enough to take a stand against Nonna?"

"I feel strong enough to hoist the Statue of Liberty in one hand," Elizabeth said, "if you're just with us, Mary Fred. I was thinking about it coming home. I'm going to dress the little mister in the clothes we made for him and that Johnny got for him. I'm going to fix up my own old clothes—"

Beany, still holding the baby in one arm and with the other hand pulling the blanket tight about him, stood staring through the rain toward the corner where the street car had just stopped to let off some passengers. "That old man that got off looks like Emerson Worth, doesn't he? Only he's got three little kids with him."

"I wish Emerson would come out," Johnny said, walking up and down the porch in his old restless, energetic way. "We ought to get to work on our book."

Mary Fred went on, "We'll make it clear to Nonna that she's welcome here, but that we've got to go ahead and be on our own, the way we always were."

"I don't know whether we can or not," Beany said unhappily. "I thought *I* could—but now—I'm not sure—" She lowered her head on top of the baby, who was almost invisible in the blankets and shawls. She pulled a corner of the rabbit blanket to her face, trying to stem the heavy aftermath of earlier sobs. "It does something to you to be shut up in a room—that's what I mean. She has so many ways of—of making you do what she wants you to."

18

Small Strangers in a Big Land

ONCE again Elizabeth stood over Beany and patted her racking shoulders and murmured in aching sympathy, "Oh, Beany—Beany, blessed, don't cry!" But with Beany's words and Beany's grief, a heavy pall of indecisiveness fell over the group on the porch with the rain crowding them close to the door. Elizabeth had said it rightly, "She has so much strength."

Johnny had tramped to the end of the porch. He exclaimed, "My gosh, that *is* Emerson Worth with those three children. And no umbrella—no nothing!"

At the gate old Emerson tried to hurry a little boy, but Mary Fred saw that the little fellow's legs were about to fold with weakness. She dashed out, scooped him up in her arms. She tried to help on the two others. One, a long-legged, sober-eyed little girl in a limp hat, was struggling with suitcases and bundles, and Johnny and Ander hurried out to take them from her.

Emerson Worth, looking more than ever like a wet old rooster, was carrying more packages and holding the hand of a very small boy, whose shoestrings flapped wetly on the sidewalk and who wore a most radiant, untroubled smile, as though rain and bundles and strange places and people were all a wondrous delight to him.

They all reached the haven of the porch. Emerson Worth took one panting breath and leaned heavily upon Elizabeth's arm which she held out to him. He managed to say, "Your father sent these little children from Hawaii to you to take care of."

Johnny gasped, "My gosh!" and Mary Fred and Elizabeth said in unison, "Father—sent them—to us!" and Beany said with a look at the one Mary Fred was sliding to the floor, "Here's my handkerchief—wipe his nose."

The long-legged little girl said casually as she walked past the baby buggy, "Over there they carried guns in baby buggies under the blankets."

Mary Fred's one desire as she looked at her was to take off that soiled and limp ruffled dress, which went so incongruously with the sweater and the heavy shoes and the poor haircut, and put warm dry clothes upon her. "Come into the house, all of you," Mary Fred urged, opening the door.

In the hall Emerson Worth took inventory of the heterogeneous collection of baggage. "We didn't forget anything, did we, Marcella?"

"No," she said tensely.

Mary Fred turned her immediate attention to the weak-kneed little boy she had carried in. She unzipped the lumberjacket he wore. Someone—it must have been Emerson Worth—had knotted a white scarf around his neck, hoping to hide the fact that no blouse was under the lumberjacket. Mary Fred smiled into his dejected face, asked, "You feel all right now, Bud?"

The smallest one with the large and radiant smile imparted this information: "A lady gave him a banana and he threw up on her shoe."

Emerson Worth said, "Marcella, give them the letter Martie Malone sent them."

Mary Fred read the penciled message on the folded piece of copy paper, with Elizabeth and Johnny and Beany crowding close to read it, too.

> We're having to rush like everything to get them on the boat. I know you'll take in these three and make them happy till I get back and can plan for them. They haven't had a father since December 7, and their mother is in the hospital.
>
> > God bless you all,
> > Father
>
> P.S. Take a picture of them and send it to their mother—they have the address. She'll rest happier if she sees it and knows they're safe with you.

A word in the last sentence had been crossed out and the word "rest" written over it. Perhaps the two words meant somewhat the same. Mary Fred realized that the first word had been "die."

Elizabeth dropped down on her knees and drew the wet, bedraggled, bewildered children into her arms. Her face was rapt and tender. "It's an answer to my prayer," she said. "I wanted to do something out of happiness and gratitude. Because I heard from Don today and he's safe. All last night I lay awake, afraid he was in a convoy that was attacked—but his letter came this morning from some place in Alaska. I knelt in church today and promised God I'd do all I could for some that weren't so blessed as my own little fellow. And now these little tykes are sent to us. What's your name, cutey?" she asked the round-faced one with the seraphic smile.

"Anthony James Bidinger," he chanted, and then added another highlight of the trip, "Marcella bit a man on the ship."

Marcella neither confirmed nor denied this, but said anxiously, "I think you'd better take the picture—like he said in the letter."

Mary Fred smiled to herself. Then Marcella had read the letter. Her father had been right to cross out that word, though it was probably little use trying to hide things from Marcella. Realism had made her eyes pitifully old for ten.

Ander ran across the yard to get his aunt's camera, because it would take pictures indoors on even such a gray day. The dog Red insisted on getting in the picture. It was his one consuming vanity, his insistence on being in every picture. It was no feat to get Anthony James to smile, and Marcella, for picture purposes, fixed a businesslike one on her face, but it wasn't until Ander said, "Now look at the bird," and Johnny made what he thought was a tweet-tweet, but which sounded more like the toot of a toy train, that Brother, of the banana incident, smiled shakily.

The minute the camera clicked, Marcella said, "I'm glad we got the picture. Because Brother has spots."

"What kind of spots?" Elizabeth asked.

"Spots. They came out the last day we were on the boat. I didn't tell the doctor because I was afraid he wouldn't let us get off. You know how funny they are about spots."

With that the Malones took over. Brother must be put to bed. Mary Fred led him upstairs. His hand, which he reached up to her, was hot and limp; his damp clothes smelled sour. Johnny telephoned to Dr. Hunter and left word at his office for him to call and diagnose the spots.

Brother was holding onto Mary Fred's hand and muttering incoherently, "He said you had a horse—and you'd let me ride the horse—he said it was the nicest horse—" And through all the hurried confusion Mary Fred felt anew that sharp pang of helplessness that had stabbed through her when she saw her Mr. Chips plodding ahead of a plow in soggy mud.

Beany was hustling Elizabeth's baby upstairs and into his room, uneasy because of Brother's spots. And Hattie had come to the fore and was wondering if the children were hungry. They were.

Then matters were further complicated. There was the rattle of an old car in front and a loud, little-boyish voice with a Cockney accent calling out, "Mary Fred—Mary Fred, will you step out here and tell the old fellow it's all right for us to stop here till tomorrow? Tell him you said we could come—before Lorna bawls her head off."

Mary Fred hurried to the door. Jock was trying to help the bewildered old Charley up the wet steps. The old man's body was drawn and stiff with arthritis. And Lorna, her face shining redly both from its hurried scrubbing and from many tears, came lugging her bushel basket. Old Charley said, "I couldn't put them off any longer. I've had no peace the whole day. They've been looking for you to come after them.

They said you told them to come in because the Easter rabbit was related to your big, white rabbit named George——"

"Frank," Lorna corrected.

Mary Fred felt conscious-stricken. "Why, yes—yes, of course I want them. We haven't dyed the eggs yet."

Jock said masterfully, "So you go on to your clinic, Uncle Charley, and tell them to give you some pain-killer. And you, Lorna, stop your bellering. Just as I've told you all day, if Mary Fred said we can come and stay all night—we can stay."

Mary Fred had to help the old man into his car. "When it rains," he muttered, breathing with pain-wrenched care, "I'm all in knots." He looked at the children, shook his head. "There's never any going back on a promise you make children. Sometimes I'm driven to promise them something to put them off from their tormenting of me, but ah, they never let me forget it."

Mary Fred rose to the occasion, assured him and the children, "We're awfully glad they came." But inner misgivings filled her. Now where could they put Brother with his spots so that none of the others came in contact with him? And what would Nonna say with five little refugees underfoot—besides the bushel basket which Lorna carried about, still optimistic, it seemed, of finding one or more "teeny-weeny" rabbits.

Dr. Hunter telephoned them and said to get Brother to bed, to keep him isolated in a warm room until he could find time to come out and examine him. Dr. Hunter, who knew the house well, said, "Put him there in your guest room. It's quiet and warm and has running water, in case he's in for a dose of something."

Nonna occupied the guest room now. But the doctor's

orders were to put Brother there. With something halfway between satisfaction and trepidation, Beany and Mary Fred hurriedly removed Nonna's toilet articles from the dresser, some of her clothes from the closet. They stood indeterminedly in the hall with them in their arms. Beany said, "My room is full," and her undertone said, "Thank heaven." "I'm taking little Lorna ︿nd Marcella in with me. And the two little boys—Jock a..d Anthony James—can sleep on the extra bed in Johnny's room. I guess Nonna will have to take Father's room."

"I guess she will," Mary Fred agreed and they carried her things in there.

When Mother died three years ago, Father had given over their two-room suite to the girls and he had moved into this small front room. The family called it the igloo, because it never heated well. It was a neat crowded room, with his closed roll-top desk, a bookcase with his special books, and a shabby black leather chair with sprawling arms.

Nonna's clothes, with their clinging perfume, and her feminine toilet articles seemed not to belong here in this man's room, with its smell of pipes, its lack of furbelows, its masculine comfort. And the very reticence and honesty of the room seemed to resent them. Uneasily Mary Fred and Beany deposited them on the bed with its dark spread.

Brother came in, anxiously searching for Mary Fred, and slid his hand into hers. She guided him back to his warmer room. Among all the people Brother clung to her. She had run out and picked him up when his knees were wabbly under him, she had smiled a reassuring welcome. Only Mary Fred could undress him; only Mary Fred could wash his hot face and hands; only for Mary Fred would he hold a thermometer under his tongue.

The whole upstairs was a furor of activity: making up the extra cot in Johnny's room, measuring little Lorna and finding she would still fit Beany's outgrown baby bed up in the attic, and bringing the bed down and setting it up in Beany's room. Hattie helped and Ander helped, and it was a bustling, hard-breathing, shin-scraping time. Ander had to leave when the beds were set up. He'd promised to pick all the tulips and hyacinths for his aunt so she could take them to church.

Then much rummaging through the linen closet for small pillows and the cases to fit them. Once Johnny murmured to Mary Fred, "Wonder what Nonna will say?"

Hattie was bending over, trying to patch together the shoelace in Anthony James' shoe. She straightened and said solemnly, "Let me tell you something; don't give in an inch to her—not an inch. If you don't, you'll be all right. It's too late for me," she said heavily. "Something's gone from me now. But it's not too late for you."

Nonna came home in high good humor, laden with purchases and more plans for her Easter entertaining. She stopped and looked disparagingly at the assorted baggage spilled in the hall. She looked disapprovingly at Lorna coming through the narrow side door and having a time of it getting herself and her bushel basket through.

"We have guests, Nonna," Mary Fred said. "Lorna and Jock came in to help dye Easter eggs. They seem to think we have a stand-in with the Easter rabbit because of Frank—" Mary Fred laughed—"but I think that bushel basket would tax any rabbit's generosity."

"*They* surely didn't bring this awful array of luggage?"

"No, we have more children. Father sent us three from Hawaii."

Elizabeth said in a low voice, "Their father was killed in the Pearl Harbor attack and their mother is in the hospital. Sweet old Dad, gathering them up and sending those poor kids here. He wired Emerson Worth and he met them and brought them out." She didn't add, though she might have, "And left, the poor fellow, before you got home."

Nonna disposed of her packages thoughtfully. She took off her rain cape and asked Hattie to wipe it dry. Slowly she took off her hat and gloves. She asked, "Was it two little girls and a boy that came from Hawaii?"

"No," Mary Fred corrected, "the oldest is a girl, Marcella, and the other two are boys."

Mary Fred saw that Nonna had a pencil and a pad of paper in her hand when she went into the telephone closet under the stairs and closed the door against the confusion of the house.

She was in the telephone closet for quite a time. She was her most ingratiating, smiling self when she emerged and came up the stairs. Mary Fred was combing Marcella's tangled hair and Elizabeth, down on her knees, was rummaging through a window seat, hoping to find an outgrown dress of Beany's for her.

Nonna gave a satisfied sigh. "Well, I finally got that worked out. It's so much better to get these children settled right away. And so—"

Two things happened simultaneously. The telephone pealed and Beany went to answer it, and someone thumped vigorously on the front door, then pushed it open with easy familiarity. "But hi, Mary Fred!"

The smell of a cigarette as well as her own thudding heart told Mary Fred it was Dike Williams. She started down the stairs, the hairbrush in her hand. "I'm surprised —but am I!" she said flusteredly. It took a longer moment than usual for her to switch back into the flippant girl of Dike's preference, because she had been so engrossed in seeing how Marcella's brown hair would look with the top braided—with maybe bangs—and the rest evened off and curled.

Dike said, "All sorts of things cooking. Our game out of town this eve is the last one—so the lid is off. Coach's wife is going along and all the team and their babes are jumping the gun on the Easter outing. We're going right up to the mountain lodge after the game. We can dance till the wee small."

"Oh! Oh!" Mary Fred spoke out of her surprise. "You're going up to the mountain lodge this evening!"

"Basketball game first. So you're going with me just as soon as you can get into the glad rags."

Mary Fred looked around helplessly. "Oh, but Dike— I'm like the old woman who lived in a shoe and had so many children and everyone needs to be washed and combed and fed and bedded down."

Nonna said, "Nonsense, Mary Fred! Of course you can go. I've made all arrangements for the children. These poor tired little things from Hawaii will be cared for better than we could here."

Beany broke in, "Mary Fred, that was Miss Hewlitt that telephoned. She wants you to call her back. 'Cause she sure is up a stump. The doctor at the clinic ordered old Charley to the hospital, his arthritis is so bad. So he can't take care of Lorna and Jock, and Miss Hewlitt already has her ticket bought to leave Monday morning for Omaha for the—oh, some kind of teachers' convention."

Mary Fred didn't answer and Beany hurried on, her eyes never leaving Mary Fred's face, "And this is what Miss Hewlitt said. She said she didn't want to impose on you, Mary Fred, but if you'd take care of the children during vacation, she'd pay you for their trouble. She said she'd insist on doing it. And she'd make it worth your while. She said for you to call her back and let her know. You will keep them, won't you, Mary Fred?"

Nonna laughed merrily. "I never heard of anything so fantastic. If Miss Hewlitt has to go off to a convention, that's her problem, not ours. She can't expect a household to upset all its program. What's her number, Beany? I'll telephone her. The same taxi that takes these children out to their Homes can take them back to Miss Hewlitt."

"To their Homes," Elizabeth echoed. "You don't mean to Homes for orphans?"

"You're not going to send them to Homes?" Beany challenged. "Father sent them to *us*."

Nonna said, "St. Clara's Orphanage told me over the telephone they would be willing to take the little girl. I had a harder time at St. Vincent's. At first they said they were full to capacity but when I told them who I was and what substantial donations I made, they consented to take the little boys. That's why we keep up orphanages—because they function in time of just such an emergency."

Dike Williams said, "Let's get rollin', babe. Coach's wife said for you gals to wear warm clothes and ear muffs and galoshes on account of the chilly mountain breezes."

Mary Fred stood there on the bottom step and felt herself being pulled and torn. A tug-of-war was going on inside her. The old Mary Fred, mop-squeezer, leaner-on, versus the new Mary Fred, queen, Dike Williams' squaw. When the old Mary Fred heard Beany tell of Miss Hewlitt insisting that she'd pay for the children's care, she had known a heartening surge of hope. Mr. Chips! With money in her hand she wouldn't be so remorseful and helpless. She could buy him back. . . . But the new Mary Fred wanted to take Dike's arm and walk out the front door and into carefreeness. She wanted the adulation that went with being Dike Williams' girl. She wanted the fun of dancing with Dike. Oh, and she could wear the new tan skirt and the green wool sweater, soft as down!

Little Marcella came down the stairs. Under her partly combed hair, her face was blank with unbelieving horror. She turned anguished eyes to Mary Fred. "Does she mean *me* at St. Clara's—and Brother and Anthony James someplace else? No—no, we can't! Anthony James is still so *little*—he has to get in bed with me in the night—"

Nonna said to her brightly, "They're going to have an Easter party at St. Clara's. You'll like that. You'll get to know all the other little girls."

Marcella flattened her thin, shaky body against the wall. "We won't go," she shrilled. "That's why he said he was sending us home to you—so we'd belong in a family—so we wouldn't be scattered—so little Anthony James would have me to look after him. *He* told Mother she needn't worry about us being scattered to the four winds."

Mary Fred reached out and drew the shrinking, feardriven Marcella to her. "Stop worrying, honey. Of course you're going to stay here." . . . She could almost see the pink-camellia, black-lace Mary Fred slink away—forever defeated. . . . Mary Fred looked at Nonna, said, "Father sent them to us. And we're going to take care of them."

She felt a great surge of strength as she stood there and looked Nonna squarely in the eye. She was almost daring the soft-voiced woman to use any of her wiles on her. Nonna shrugged, started up the stairs.

And when Mary Fred had come into her own once more, Dike Williams was almost anti-climax. For her fingers longed to get back to Marcella's hair and, even as she said, "Sorry, Dike, and all that, but I guess I'll have to give some other girl a break," she was thinking of where they'd hide the Easter baskets for them all. She was wondering if they could find a "teeny-weeny" rabbit and put it in Lorna's bushel basket to surprise her. Oh, and the eggs! They ought to be on boiling now.

She was even impatient with Dike and his lingering on, trying to argue her into going. As she closed the door on him, this thought surprised her, "Why, it's more fun to be home and doing things." And still another, "It's more fun being with Ander than it is with Dike." Already her mind was storing up for recounting to Ander some of the startling things the seraphic Anthony James said. She wondered soberly, as she wet the hairbrush for finishing Marcella's hair-do, if Ander were, by now, disgusted with her. She knew a sudden ache of longing to be back on the same friendly footing with him.

Beany was getting the last word with Nonna. "They couldn't go to a Home anyway because of Brother's spots. He's in your bed."

19

From Queen to Mop-Squeezer

ON THIS Easter morning of bright warm sun, Mary Fred sat in church beside Beany and Johnny and young Marcella from Hawaii. The singing of the choir, the scent of the flower-laden altar, the poignant loveliness of the mass smoothed out the wrinkles in Mary Fred's soul.

The church was crowded. Mary Fred had to take Marcella on her lap. What a thin, long-legged bit of childhood she was! She was wearing a dress Beany had worn two or three years ago but it had never hung so loosely on Beany's stocky figure. Mary Fred whispered in her ear, "If you eat as much as Beany, you'll get as husky as she is."

Elizabeth had tiptoed out of the house and gone to an earlier service so that she could "ride herd," as Ander put it, on the small children while the other Malones went.

Mary Fred had telephoned Miss Hewlitt and told her she would look after the children during vacation. Miss Hewlitt had been nice! For when Mary Fred confessed her need for money to rescue Mr. Chips, Miss Hewlitt had said, "I'll stop by with the money for you before I leave for Omaha Monday morning. You get Mr. Chips back."

Mary Fred drew a long breath. The Malones didn't want a fairy godmother showering gifts upon them. And, come to think of it, in all those fairy stories there was always a string, a *must* attached to the gifts. Cinderella's godmother had enjoined, "You *must* be home by twelve o'clock." The dwarf, that untangled the thread, had then kept the princess in agony trying to guess that his name was *Rumpelstilzchen.* "The highest price you can pay for a thing is to get it for nothing." Johnny had paid for the new and shining typewriter with his own self-respect. Elizabeth had admitted that the new clothes, the bassinet for the baby seemed to separate her from Don and all their dreams together. And she, Mary Fred—she squirmed in anguish of self-reproach— she had been a traitor to herself, to the ones who had turned to her.

Oh, but now, now it was nice to be back in the mop-squeezer, leaner-on class where she belonged.

When they returned from church Dr. Hunter had been there to see Brother. "He thinks it isn't anything contagious," Elizabeth said. "It's a stomach rash from nerves and fatigue, he thought. But he's a pretty sick little codger. And he keeps asking for you, Mary Fred."

"I'll be right here," Mary Fred assured him.

There were two late breakfasts at the Malone home that noon. One in the dining room with a color scheme of yellow jonquils and lavender candles; even the broiled grapefruit fitted into it. That was Nonna's breakfast.

The other was out under the weeping willow in the Malone's back yard, with the warmest sun April could manage out in full force after the rain. And the color scheme of this breakfast was as reckless as nature itself. For, as fast as the children found their baskets of colored eggs, they ran to the table with them.

Only Lorna was too happily engrossed with the contents of her bushel basket to hunt for eggs. Johnny and Carlton, in their red jalopy, had gone out early this morning, had stopped at five truck farms before they found and purchased, not one, but two little black-and-white rabbits. "I hope they don't keep on growing and growing like Frank did," Beany murmured.

While Brother was sleeping, Mary Fred slipped downstairs. Old Emerson Worth was there. When breakfast was ready, Beany had had to go up to Johnny's room and pry them both away from The Book. The children took turns, guided by the Malones, at broiling bacon over the fireplace. Nonna's broiled chicken and dollar-sized biscuits monopolized the kitchen range. The outdoor breakfast party ate yesterday's bran muffins with the bacon and drank cocoa.

Breakfast was over, and Emerson Worth leaned back tiredly on the iron bench. And it was then that the old man made the greatest concession they had ever heard him make. He said, "I feel better about the world and the sorry fix it's in. You young folks do take hold. I guess bravery is just doing the job at hand."

Beany said *sotto voce*, "Giants walk Barberry Street these days."

But they felt newly humble to be compared to the heroes of yesterday.

All day Mary Fred hoped Ander would come. But he didn't.

Saturday and Sunday night Nonna slept in Father's room.

She said, "Whoever called that room an Eskimo's igloo was right. And everything in it is saturated with pipe and tobacco smell. I've heard that men like a hard, ungiving bed, but my goodness—that one!"

Mary Fred only smiled absently. She was trying hard to get over to the little farm opposite the Day-or-Night Stables to see if it was possible to buy Mr. Chips back. But all morning she and Beany washed. In the afternoon when she might have gone, Brother clung to her in sick misery.

Monday night Nonna slept in the room with Elizabeth and the baby. She said the next morning, "Elizabeth, I wonder that you can sleep with the baby's stirring so much in the night. He doesn't cry out loud but he fusses every now and then."

Beany said, "The nurse at St. Joseph's said just to let a baby do that, and he'd soon form the habit of sleeping the whole night through."

But Nonna's eyes, her movements were tired.

Beany offered, "We can fix it so you won't have to sleep either in Father's room or with Elizabeth. We can double up some more and you can have my room."

Nonna said slowly, "Thank you, Beany, but I have some half-formed plans in the back of my mind."

On Tuesday, Mary Fred took the car in which Johnny had a half-interest and drove down to the little farm. She turned off the main road, drove up a rutty lane past the field where she had seen Mr. Chips pulling a plow to the handful of low dilapidated buildings. There was no sign of Mr. Chips in the field this day. And, although Mary Fred knocked and called, she found no one at home. She poked about the place, hoping to hear a soft, familiar whinny, hop-

ing for a chance to pat the white-splashed forehead in re-
assurance. But she saw only a white horse, two red cows,
about whose feet chickens scratched and pecked.

She couldn't return the next day because the red car refused to run. Several times, in her anxiety, she looked toward
Mrs. Adams'. Ander wasn't having vacation. This was one
of his toughest weeks, he had said. Mary Fred had to take
time, between caring for Brother and ironing, to help Johnny
and Carlton trace a short in the wiring system so the car
would be drivable the following day.

Thursday afternoon she and Johnny drove again to the
place. This time the farmer was setting out cabbage plants
in his garden. He was a stolid, stupid man who spoke English brokenly.

"The black horse? Is not here—is gone."

A half-hour later Johnny took Mary Fred's arm and said,
"Come on, Mary Fred. No use asking him questions. If he's
sold the horse, he's sold it. If he doesn't know who bought
it, no use trying to find out. He says he sold it Sunday.
Maybe we can think up something. Maybe we could put
an ad in the paper."

Mary Fred sat silent and sick beside him as they drove
home. Johnny tried to divert her heavy disappointment by
saying, as they turned in their driveway, "Well—talk about
a flock of sparrows sitting on a bough!"

Marcella and little Anthony James, Lorna and Jock, even
Beany, were perched on the porch's edge. If Mary Fred
hadn't been so dulled with her own grief, she might have
noticed that each one was holding his lips shut tight, as
though he were container for something he could scarcely
contain.

With heavy feet Mary Fred started up the steps. Jock

burst out, "So you went after your black horse, did you—?" Marcella nudged him violently.

Mary Fred said bleakly, "Yes, but he was sold." Her voice thickened, "I—I'd rather not talk about it."

Beany slid off the porch and caught her sister's hand. "Don't look like that, Mary Fred. It's a surprise—but—but anyway you go look in the garage."

Before her stumbling feet could reach the garage she smelled that pungent brown liniment, and heard Ander whistling softly. A horse nickered as she opened the door. . . .

Mr. Chips was so thin. His ribs showed through his furry sides. The collar had rubbed a sore on his neck. Ander said, "His leg's swollen bad now. But we'll soon cure that."

Mary Fred took the black horse's head in her arms and sobbed out, "Oh, Chips—you ought to hate me—I failed you so—"

Once again Ander let her cry. He kept on whistling softly, shaking up the liniment, rubbing it into the swollen leg. He was telling her that he had bought the horse from the farmer on Sunday. "But he was limping so he could hardly walk. I took him to a veterinary and left him there until today."

"Will you let me buy him back from you?" Mary Fred asked humbly. "I'm back in the laboring class—not the parasite—now. I've got some money. And I'm going to make some more, somehow, so I can take care of him."

Ander said, "Why can't we own him together? That way I can boss you harder. You told me once I was bossy, you know."

Mary Fred said impulsively, "I'd like you to boss me, Ander. I'd like you to like me the way you used to."

191

Ander said gently, "Don't worry about that, Mary Fred. You know what I've been planning? That this summer we'll load old Chips on a trailer and take him up to our ranch. Maybe Elizabeth and the little mister could go up for a vacation. Would you like to or—or maybe you and this Harkness hero have other plans?"

Mary Fred laughed shakily, "I haven't got any Harkness hero and, oh gosh, Ander, it's nice not to have. It's so comfortable not to have. I didn't realize how sick I was of wisecracks. I'd love to go to your ranch. I'll talk to Elizabeth about it tonight."

And then they found themselves standing, smiling happily at each other. Ander said, "Here, you scrub out this bucket and get some water. I'll go ahead and bandage his leg."

Mary Fred brought the water. She reached for the currycomb and brush. Ander began unwinding the bandage. They were not without an audience as they worked. Jock and Lorna, Marcella and little Anthony James all watched and gave advice. Marcella said once, "If I hold Brother to the window, will you lead the black horse out for him to see?"

The nice sound of Mr. Chips munching oats, the clean smell of saddle soap. The nice way you could say to Ander, "Did I tell you about—?" Janet had said of Dike Williams, "He has charm and athletic prowess, period."

Suddenly Mary Fred said, "Ander, wait for me here. I'm going in to tell Nonna that I've got Mr. Chips back. Wait for me—I'm scared. I don't know how she'll take it."

She came back just as Ander was taping the snug bandage on Mr. Chips' leg. He grinned. "I see you're still in one piece. What'd she say?"

Mary Fred said dazedly, "Why, she didn't say anything I thought she'd say. She didn't seem to think much about it. She said she got a letter from the people that bought out her decorating business in Philadelphia, and they're having trouble getting workmen and material, and they've lost some of her best customers. She said she thought they'd be willing to have her take it back off their hands."

"H'mm," Ander said.

"And do you know what else she said? She said she was the kind of a woman who had to have her hands full of managing, and that maybe she'd better stick to color schemes and textiles, rather than other people's lives. And while I was in there Lila phoned. Private First Class Clancy was at her house and wondered if we could have the square dance here Saturday night—night after next—and I said yes, we could. You can call it for us, can't you?"

"Sure," Ander agreed. He added thoughtfully, "I wouldn't be surprised but that Nonna left tomorrow. Here, hold this can of salve, while I get some out for this sore on his neck."

The next evening, Friday, the Malones gathered around the council table. Even as Ander had predicted, Nonna and Hattie had left on the 4:45 eastbound streamliner that day.

Johnny acted as though a weight had been lifted from his shoulders. And it had. He had returned the new typewriter to the company, returned the money to Nonna, returned his old space-skipper to his blue desk and its cover to the corner. And he had started writing the Eugene Field incident, laughing with appreciation of the poetic prankster all the while he wrote.

Johnny came to the council table, breathless and unkempt. He'd had a struggle getting the little boys, Jock and Anthony James, to bed in his room. He'd had to let them take turns playing he was a bucking bronco. He panted out as he sat down.

> "Ah, what would the world be to us,
> If the children were no more!"

Johnny had other good news, too. When Mrs. Thompson came in to the dentist she brought, out of gratitude to and fondness for Johnny, several dozen eggs which were "imperfects"—some large, some small, some cracked. Johnny said mysteriously, "There might be a Lady Eleanor cake for them as appreciates it."

"How you going to use up the egg *yolks?*" Beany wanted to know.

"Could it be that you have forgotten Noodles à la Naples?"

Ander and Emerson Worth had been there to dinner and had stayed on. Emerson Worth was far back in the past again. "And then came the lean years—the panic years, and only the hardiest could stick them out. Every so often the world shakes under our feet."

Mary Fred, acting as chairman, said, "The council has a lot of unfinished business." She looked down at her notes. "Jock and Lorna" was one. Miss Hewlitt was willing to pay them generously for taking care of the two indefinitely. Old Charley was still laid up with arthritis and Miss Hewlitt had her teaching job. "Hired help" was another item. The council must talk over whether, out of their board money, they should hire full- or part-time help. Elizabeth's aureole of hair must not frame too tired a face.

Marcella was squeezed in next to Beany, whom she adored.

She hung on every word that Beany uttered. She was all eagerness to prove her worth to Beany. Beany said, "I'll take over the cooking the first third of the month by myself."

"But you'll have me to help," Marcella reminded her.

Mary Fred was just saying, "And Johnny and I will take the last twenty days," when suddenly Red, who had been sound asleep on Mary Fred's foot, hurtled up and ran to the front door with an ecstatic whine trembling through him. In another minute the door opened and a man's voice said, "Now, Red, can't I ever slip in without your knowing it!"

Johnny fell backwards, chair and all, as he yelled out, "It's Father!"

It took a good half-hour for them all to greet him, for him to see Elizabeth's baby—little Martin Donald Mac-Callin—for him to drink a glass of milk and eat three of their fresh doughnuts and tell about his airplane trip back from Hawaii.

They all moved back to the council table. Father said, looking around the table, "The fight's getting tougher. That means tougher on all of us."

He wouldn't say more than that. But they knew he meant that they must give more of themselves, their work, their money. "Yes, we know," each one nodded soberly.

Father got up. "Where's my pipe?" he asked. The pipe ritual was on. Find the pipe, tap out the old tobacco, fill it with new, and tamp it and tamp it. Where is the ash tray? Where is a match?

Mary Fred's and Ander's eyes met. She wasn't sure whether the surge that went through her, choking in her throat, was happiness or soberness. Or both.

ABOUT THE AUTHOR

Lenora Mattingly Weber was born in Dawn, Missouri. When she was twelve her adventurous family set out to homestead in Colorado. It is here that she has lived and worked ever since.

Her well-loved stories reflect her own experiences. As a mother of six and a grandmother she is well equipped to write of family life. Her love of the outdoors, her interest in community affairs, and her appreciation of warm family relationships help make the Malones as winning as they are. While Mrs. Weber gets much pleasure from cooking for her large family, her first love is writing.